PENG

THE LIFTED

MARY ANN (MARIAN) E   . She
attended schools in Nuneaton and Coventry, coming under the influence of evangelical teachers and clergymen. In 1836 her mother died
and Marian became her father's housekeeper, educating herself in her
spare time. In 1841 she moved to Coventry, and met Charles and
Caroline Bray, local progressive intellectuals. Through them she was
commissioned to translate Strauss's *Life of Jesus* and met the radical
publisher John Chapman, who, when he purchased the *Westminster*
Review in 1851, made her his managing editor. Having lost her Christian
fa

GEORGE ELIOT

The Lifted Veil *and* Brother Jacob

Edited with an Introduction and Notes by
SALLY SHUTTLEWORTH

PENGUIN BOOKS

PENGUIN BOOKS

Published by the Penguin Group
Penguin Books Ltd, 27 Wrights Lane, London w8 5TZ, England
Penguin Putnam Inc., 375 Hudson Street, New York, New York 10014, USA
Penguin Books Australia Ltd, Ringwood, Victoria, Australia
Penguin Books Canada Ltd, 10 Alcorn Avenue, Toronto, Ontario, Canada M4V 3B2
Penguin Books India (P) Ltd, 11, Community Centre, Panchsheel Park, New Delhi – 110 017, India
Penguin Books (NZ) Ltd, Private Bag 102902, NSMC, Auckland, New Zealand
Penguin Books (South Africa) (Pty) Ltd, 5 Watkins Street, Denver Ext 4, Johannesburg 2094, South Africa

Penguin Books Ltd, Registered Offices: Harmondsworth, Middlesex, England

'The Lifted Veil' first published 1859; 'Brother Jacob' first published 1864
Published in Penguin Classics 2001

1

Introduction and Notes copyright © Sally Shuttleworth, 2001
All rights reserved

The moral right of the editor has been asserted

Set in 10/12 pt Monotype Janson
Typeset by Rowland Phototypesetting Ltd, Bury St Edmunds, Suffolk
Printed in England by Clays Ltd, St Ives plc

CONTENTS

ACKNOWLEDGEMENTS

My thanks are due to Gowan Dawson, Simon Goldhill, Louise Henson and Jonathan Topham for their invaluable scholarly aid, and to Oliver Christie for the illustrations.

There have been two previous annotated editions of these stories, Peter Mudford's for Everyman (1996) and Helen Small's for Oxford World's Classics (1999). I am indebted to both these works.

BIBLIOGRAPHICAL NOTE

Essays   Thomas Pinney (ed.), *Essays of George Eliot* (New York: Columbia University Press, 1963).

Journals   Margaret Harris and Judith Johnston (eds.), *The Journals of George Eliot* (Cambridge: Cambridge University Press, 1998).

Letters   Gordon S. Haight (ed.), *George Eliot Letters*, 9 vols. (New Haven: Yale University Press, 1954–78).

Lewes Ms Journal G. H. Lewes Ms Journals, Beinecke Rare Book and Manuscript Library, Yale University.

1819   *22 November*, born at Arbury, Warwickshire.

1824–36 Attends boarding schools in Attleborough, Nuneaton and Coventry.

1836   *3 February*, mother dies.

1837   After sister Christiana marries, becomes father's housekeeper. Commences a lifetime programme of wide reading.

1841   Moves with her father to Coventry where she meets Charles and Caroline ('Cara') Bray. Reads Charles Hennell's *An Inquiry Concerning the Origin of Christianity* (1838) which leads her to question her religious faith.

1842   *January–May*, the 'Holy War' with her father when she refuses to attend church. Beginning of friendship with Charles Hennell and his sister Sara.

1844   Begins a translation of Strauss's *Das Leben Jesu* (4th edn., 1840). *July*, travels to London with Charles Bray to have a phrenological cast taken of her head.

1846   *The Life of Jesus* published.

1846–7 'Poetry and Prose, from the Notebook of an Eccentric', published in the Coventry *Herald and Observer*.

1847–8 Nurses father.

1848   *July*, meets Ralph Waldo Emerson.

1849   Begins to translate Spinoza's *Tractatus theologico-politicus*. *31 May*, death of father. *June*, sets off for France, Italy and Switzerland with the Brays; they return to England in July. Remains in Geneva, lodging, from *October*, with the painter M. D'Albert-Durade and his wife. Begins journal.

1850   *March*, M. D'Albert-Durade escorts her back to London. Feels unwanted by her family and resides with the Brays. Decides to earn her living by writing. *October*, visits John Chapman in London.

1851   *January*, her first major article, 'The Progress of the Intellect', published in the *Westminster Review. September*, moves to London and becomes assistant editor of the *Westminster*. Meets Herbert Spencer and George Henry Lewes.

1852   *January*, her first number of the *Westminster* published. Close friendship with Spencer. *October*, visits the phrenological theorist George Combe in Edinburgh.

1853   Working hard on the *Westminster*. *October*, intimacy with Lewes begins.

1854   *July*, translation of Feuerbach's *Essence of Christianity* published. Leaves for Germany with Lewes. Begins translation of Spinoza's *Ethics*.

1855   *March*, returns to England with Lewes, and they set up house together.

1856   Trips to Ilfracombe and Tenby to collect materials for Lewes's *Sea-side Studies* (1858). Begins to write fiction, 'The Sad Fortunes of Amos Barton'. 'The Natural History of German Life' and 'Silly Novels by Lady Novelists', published in the *Westminster*.

1857   'Amos Barton', 'Mr Gilfil's Love-Story' and 'Janet's Repentance', published in *Blackwood's Edinburgh Magazine*. Assumes pseudonym, George Eliot. Writes to her brother of her relationship with Lewes and he breaks off communication. Further marine biology trips to Jersey and the Scilly Isles. Rumours of Joseph Liggins's authorship of Eliot's stories start to circulate. *October*, begins *Adam Bede*.

1858   *January, Scenes of Clerical Life*. Travels with Lewes to Munich, then to Dresden via Salzburg, Vienna and Prague.

1859   *February, Adam Bede. April*, interrupts composition of *The Mill on the Floss* to write 'The Lifted Veil', published in *Blackwood's* in *July. June*, pressured into unveiling the identity of 'George Eliot'.

1860   *April, The Mill on the Floss*. Trip to Italy where she conceives the idea of *Romola. August*, writes 'Brother Jacob'. Begins *Silas Marner*.

1861   *April, Silas Marner*. Further trip to Italy for research on *Romola* which she starts to write in *October*.

1862   *July, Romola* begins serialization in *Cornhill Magazine*.

1863   *July, Romola*. She and Lewes buy the Priory, Regent's Park.

1864   Begins verse play *The Spanish Gypsy. July*, 'Brother Jacob', published in the *Cornhill*.

1865   *February*, temporarily abandons her verse play which is making her ill. *March*, starts writing *Felix Holt*.

1866   *June, Felix Holt.* Returns to work on *The Spanish Gypsy*.

1867   Trip to Spain to collect material. Subscribes £50 to the foundation of Girton College, Cambridge.

1868   *May, The Spanish Gypsy.*

1869   Writes 'Brother and Sister' sonnets, and begins *Middlemarch*.

1870   'The Legend of Jubal', published in *Macmillan's Magazine*.

1871   'Armgart', published in *Macmillan's*.

1871–2   *Middlemarch* published in eight parts.

1874   *The Legend of Jubal and Other Poems.*

1876   *Daniel Deronda*, published in eight parts. Purchases the Heights in Witley, Surrey.

1878   *30 November*, Lewes dies.

1879   Preparing last volume of Lewes's *Problems of Life and Mind* for publication. *The Impressions of Theophrastus Such.*

1880   *6 May*, marries John Walter Cross. *22 December*, dies in London.

INTRODUCTION

*Note: New readers are advised that this Introduction
makes the detail of the plots explicit.*

'The Lifted Veil'

In 'The Lifted Veil' George Eliot solves one of the most difficult narrative conundrums: how to narrate one's own death. First-person narratives can normally take us to the point where death seems imminent: where the assassin enters the room, or pain causes the writing to falter, but they cannot take us further, to the actual moment of death. As readers we can only assume an abrupt cessation of narrative has been caused by death, we can never follow our narrator into death itself. In 'The Lifted Veil', however, Eliot overcomes that problem by endowing her narrator, Latimer, with prevision. He lives, over and over again, the moment of his own future death. The ominous opening of the tale, 'The time of my end approaches', sets the scene for a story where the future is entirely foreclosed. In a sense, what we are offered is a posthumous narrative, for we are plunged immediately into Latimer's account of his death, with full circumstantial and physical details: the failure of the servants to attend, the mounting pain and emotional despair, and finally,

Darkness – darkness – no pain – nothing but darkness: but I am passing on and on through the darkness: my thought stays in the darkness, but always with a sense of moving onward.... (ch. 1)

At what point does death occur? Have we passed through death and out the other side, but only to be met by unending darkness? The answer is left to our imagination.

Latimer is the very opposite of Scheherezade in *The Arabian Nights*, who postpones her death by enthralling the Sultan with her stories. Where her narration maintains the possibility of hope, development

and survival, Latimer's circular narrative charts only his painful movement towards the already enacted moment of his death, a moment
which is for him already a part of memory. The pen drops from his
hand in the final line of the tale as his vision of his own death is fulfilled.
No impersonal narrator is required to finish the story: the life of the
narrative is coterminous with that of the narrator.

The endings of stories and novels usually create a network of further
speculations; as George Eliot noted in the Finale to *Middlemarch*
(1871–2): 'Every limit is a beginning as well as an ending.' This generaliz-
ation does not hold true, however, for 'The Lifted Veil'. No room is
offered for further speculation; as readers, for example, we have no
concerns as to what might happen to Bertha in the future. Our attention,
like that of Latimer, is narrowed down to a single point: our only
possible movement forward is to relive, like Latimer, the moment of
his death once more. Like the Wedding Guest in Coleridge's poem,
we are trapped by this self-absorbed version of an Ancient Mariner,
shut off from present and future as we are locked within the repetitive
cycle of the tale.

A 'jeu de melancolie'

'The Lifted Veil' was written in the first months of 1859, alongside the
first chapters of *The Mill on the Floss*. Eliot records in her journal for 26
April 1859: 'Finished a story – "The Lifted Veil" – which I began one
morning at Richmond as a resource when my head was too stupid
for more important work.'[1] She had written to her publisher, John
Blackwood, on 31 March, to let him know that she was at work on a
new novel which would be 'a sort of companion picture of provincial
life' for *Adam Bede*, but then proceeded to offer him 'a slight story of an
outré kind – not a *jeu d'esprit*, but a *jeu de melancolie*' for his magazine: 'I
think nothing of it, but my private critic [G. H. Lewes] says it is very
striking and original, and on the strength of that opinion, I mention
it.'[2] Blackwood's reception of the tale was far from rapturous, however;
although he remained courteous as ever in his responses, and published
the story in the July issue of *Blackwood's Edinburgh Magazine*, he resisted
the suggestion that George Eliot's name should be attached to it.[3] He
commented privately to his brother that 'I thought it better not to

fritter away the prestige which should be kept fresh for the new novel.'⁴ Since rumour was rife throughout Britain at this time as to the authorship of those literary sensations *Scenes of Clerical Life* and *Adam Bede*, Blackwood's decision to forgo an instant boost to his magazine's circulation figures signals his real disappointment with the tale. In place of the warm humanity and moral stance of these earlier works, Eliot's story offered a cold, egotistical first-person narrator, who found nothing but spite and pettiness around him.

Blackwood was quick to identify the misery of Latimer with the state of Eliot's mind during composition: 'I wish the theme had been a happier one, and I think you must have been worrying and disturbing yourself about something when you wrote.'⁵ The tale is self-reflexive with regard to Eliot's own life, but also to her role as writer. The narrative structure creates an indivisibility between text and voice, for the end of the text also marks the death of its author. Latimer is granted the gifts George Eliot deemed crucial to narrative art: an ability to enter into the minds of others, and the power to foresee the future. The first lies behind Eliot's doctrine of sympathy, as outlined in *Adam Bede* and 'The Natural History of German Life' (1856): 'Art is the nearest thing to life; it is a mode of amplifying experience and extending our contact with our fellow-men beyond the bounds of our personal lot.'⁶ Shortly after completing 'The Lifted Veil', Eliot defined this artistic position with even greater forcefulness in a letter to her friend Charles Bray:

If Art does not enlarge men's sympathies, it does nothing morally.

I have had heart-cutting experience that opinions are a poor cement between human souls; and the only effect I ardently long to produce by my writings, is that those who read them should be better able to *imagine* and to *feel* the pains and the joys of those who differ from themselves in everything but the broad fact of being struggling erring human creatures.⁷

Latimer has this power to experience the emotions and thoughts of others, but the effect is the very reverse of the extension of sympathy. Insight, for Latimer, brings revulsion. His power of prevision also links him to the role of author, extending imagination into the future in order to construct the movements of characters and plot. Yet for Latimer both these writerly gifts are curses.

'Writing', Eliot observed in 1857, 'is part of my religion.'⁸ In this 'jeu de melancolie' she seems to create a narrative world which reverses all the tenets of her secular religion, while simultaneously cutting off hope for a transcendental afterlife. Far from opening up new worlds, or creating visions of potentiality, the tale narrows down its perspective to the interstices of the individual mind, creating an unbearable sense of claustrophobia. The only form of rebirth, or afterlife, portrayed is that generated by the macabre scientific experiment where blood is transfused into the corpse of Mrs Archer, endowing her only with the power to curse before she dies a second time.

John Blackwood had objected strongly to the revivification scene and asked that it be removed. Eliot refused. It is not merely an optional detail, included for sensational effect, but an integral part of the tale's conceptual structure. Blackwood was correct in his surmise, however, that 'some of our excellent scientific friend's experiments on some confounded animalcule' lay behind the revivification experiment.[9] Eliot was writing 'The Lifted Veil' in a domestic context of scientific experimentation. Her partner, George Henry Lewes, was busy with his vivisection of frogs, and writing *The Physiology of Common Life*, one of the most influential works in the emerging science of physiological psychology. Although Eliot's tale seems to brush with the supernatural, its language throughout belongs firmly to the world of contemporary science. 'The Lifted Veil' can be seen, indeed, as a meditation on the role of art in relation to the new definitions of life and death offered by a materialist science of body and mind. In many ways it continues the trains of thought of its famous predecessor, Mary Shelley's *Frankenstein* (1818), which was also partially set in Geneva.

Unusually for an Eliot text, 'The Lifted Veil' is placed very precisely in time: Latimer's death occurs on 20 September 1850. In Eliot's own life this date coincides with her return from Geneva, where she, like Latimer, had spent some time, and her subsequent anxious attempts to define a pathway in life now that her father's death had released her from domestic obligations. Unfortunately, Eliot's journal for this period was destroyed by the husband of her final years, John Cross, in his efforts to maintain the image of her he wished to pass down to posterity.[10] Similarly, her great friend in Geneva, the painter François D'Albert-Durade in whose house she had lodged, also destroyed her letters of this period. The few remaining letters from these months do suggest, however, a bleak time in her life. She clearly felt rejected by her brother, Isaac Evans, when she returned, and wrote to her friend Sara Hennell on 11 April: 'It was some envious demon that drove me across the Jura to come and see people who don't want me. However I am determined to sell everything I possess except a portmanteau and carpet-bag and the necessary contents and be a stranger and a foreigner on the earth for ever more.'[11] Such sentiments are echoed in the conclusion of 'The Lifted Veil', where Latimer becomes a lonely 'wanderer in foreign countries', cut off from all human sympathies. Eliot's brother had concurred with her father's suspicions of her free-thinking friends the Hennells and the Brays, and no doubt thoroughly disapproved of her current lifestyle. Eliot, or Marian Evans as she then was, had cast aside her religion at great personal cost, and spurned the customary female path of domesticity, but was yet to find a sense of vocation that could give new meaning to her life.

In 1859 Eliot was suffering from the consequences of her anonymity being breached. Friends had become in her eyes figures to be distrusted, 'false and narrow-hearted', subject to 'envy, hatred, or malice' and liable to betray secrets.[12] She had become even more sensitive to the difficulties of her position as writer, difficulties intensified both by her sex and her anomalous social position as the unmarried partner of Lewes. Her sister, Chrissey, after following Isaac's example and cutting off communication with Eliot, had sent a letter in March 1859 to say that she wanted to heal the breach, but this was swiftly followed by news of her death. Eliot wrote to Sara Hennell on 21 March that 'Chrissey's death has taken from the possibility of many things towards which I looked with some hope and yearning in the future.'[13] The despair that usually accompanied her ending one work and starting a new was intensified by this unexpected foreclosing of the future.

In her private journal for 2 January 1858 Eliot had welcomed the positive reviews of her first fictional work, *Scenes of Clerical Life*, as 'indications that I can touch the hearts of my fellow men, and so sprinkle some precious grain as the result of the long years in which I have been inert and suffering'.[14] Readerly response offered her a means of self-validation, not merely of her creative powers, but also of what she viewed (perversely one might feel) as the 'inertness' of her previous life. In a similar vein, she wrote to Blackwood, less than two weeks after finishing 'The Lifted Veil': 'Yes – I *am* assured now that "Adam Bede" was worth writing – worth living through long years to write.

But now it seems impossible to me that I shall ever write anything so good and true again. I have arrived at faith in the past, but not at faith in the future.'[15] Success has brought a retrospective valuation of past life, but increased the burdens placed upon the future. Eliot's earlier loss of religious faith dominates all her creative work. Once death ceases to be the transition to a higher life, and becomes absolute, the quest for meaning in this life becomes almost intolerable (as manifested in Eliot's interminable headaches). With the collapse of her faith, Eliot's Protestant quest for justification became even more intense, while she remained resolute in her refusal of the '*opium*' offered by belief in an afterlife.[16] The 'weight of my future life' exerts an almost paralysing pressure.[17] Writing takes on a moral urgency which threatens to destroy its object. Eliot had long meditated a work on the 'Idea of a Future Life':[18] in many ways 'The Lifted Veil' is the negative reflection of that plan.

Death and desire

For Lewes, science was to offer the answer to the void left by religion: 'Onward, and for ever onward, mightier and for ever mightier, rolls this wondrous tide of discovery' bringing a constant progress towards higher social development.[19] Following the French philosopher Auguste Comte (1798–1857), he believed that 'Science gives the power to *foresee*, and *foreseeing* leads to *action*. Hence the relation of Science and Art'.[20] But what if the power to foresee led not to action, but to paralysis? Eliot's tale explores not the power of knowledge, but its powerlessness. Space, she suggests, must be left for the workings of desire. Latimer's attraction to Bertha is based on the fact that she possesses the only mind which remains closed to his powers of penetration:

no matter how empty the adytum,[21] so that the veil be thick enough. So absolute is our soul's need of something hidden and uncertain for the maintenance of that doubt and hope and effort which are the breath of its life, that if the whole future were laid bare to us beyond to-day, the interest of all mankind would be bent on the hours that lie between; we should pant after the uncertainties of our one morning and our one afternoon; we should rush fiercely to the

Exchange for our last possibility of speculation, of success, of disappointment; we should have a glut of political prophets foretelling a crisis or a no-crisis within the only twenty-four hours left open to prophecy. Conceive the condition of the human mind if all propositions whatsoever were self-evident except one, which was to become self-evident at the close of a summer's day, but in the meantime might be the subject of question, of hypothesis, of debate. Art and philosophy, literature and science, would fasten like bees on that one proposition which had the honey of probability in it, and be the more eager because their enjoyment would end with sunset. Our impulses, our spiritual activities, no more adjust themselves to the idea of their future nullity, than the beating of our heart, or the irritability of our muscles. (ch. 2)

Eliot[22] scans the entire scale of human endeavour, bringing us at last to the physiological bedrock of all, and quite specifically the current area of Lewes's scientific work: the irritability of muscles. Human life in this vision appears simultaneously noble and pathetic: all efforts to 'pant' after the unknown are levelled, whether they be financial speculation on the Exchange, high philosophy or lust for the concealed mysteries of womanhood. For desire to operate, Eliot suggests, there must be two conditions: an element of the unknown and the threat of death. Without that fear of termination, desire would remain dormant.

Like Milton, Eliot believed the world of human effort and endeavour is only made possible by a constant awareness of death.[23] In her 1869 poem 'The Legend of Jubal', she would return once more to these themes, offering her own extension of *Paradise Lost*. Cain, at the opening of the poem, has fled to a new land, hoping to shake off the threat of death. His people live in 'soft idlesse' until death strikes:

> Now glad Content by clutching Haste was torn,
> And Work grew eager, and Device was born.[24]

Ambition and passion now throb through their veins, as the awareness of death gives new value to time, and the newly awakened soul finds its highest expression in music, the invention of Jubal. Creative art, Eliot suggests, is only possible when death is 'lord of Life'. Yet Jubal himself cannot reap the benefits of his fame: returning after long years away, he is beaten and thrust out of the community for daring to claim that he is the god they now worship. In a transparent comment on her own position, Eliot suggests the artist must be prepared to be personally reviled:

> Thy limbs shall lie dark, tombless on this sod,
> Because thou shinest in man's soul, a god . . .
> 'Twas but in giving that thou couldst atone
> For too much wealth amid their poverty.[25]

Eliot returned repeatedly to the role of the artist in her work, and to his or her relations to the rest of humanity.[26] In this formulation, the power of artistic genius in endorsed, but at the expense of the 'poverty'-stricken listening audience.

Unlike Jubal, Latimer will leave no creative legacy, while his knowledge of the precise time and circumstances of his death has taken away death's power to energize. He possesses, he believes, 'the poet's sensibility without his voice' (ch. 1). He had at first welcomed his vision of the city of Prague: 'was it the poet's nature in me, hitherto only a troubled yearning sensibility, now manifesting itself suddenly as spontaneous creation?' He is soon to be disillusioned. Whereas a poet 'pours forth his song and *believes* in the listening ear and answering soul', Latimer is destined to feel only scorn for the listening ear. Art, Eliot suggests, is dependent on an audience; an artist must believe that an audience will listen and respond in kind, with 'an answering soul'. Without that anticipatory belief, creative vision becomes merely a 'diseased' form of consciousness.

Diseased vision

When granted the power of vision to see into the minds of others, Latimer fails to find an answering soul:

the rational talk, the graceful attentions, the wittily-turned phrases, and the kindly deeds, which used to make the web of their characters, were seen as if thrust asunder by a microscopic vision, that showed all the intermediate frivolities, all the suppressed egoism, all the struggling chaos of puerilities, meanness, vague capricious memories, and indolent make-shift thoughts, from which human words and deeds emerge like leaflets covering a fermenting heap. (ch. 1)

Under Latimer's microscopic analysis we find, not the glories of nature, but the complexities of human consciousness reduced to the rotting vegetation of a compost heap. That sensitivity to the inner life, so much prized in the rest of Eliot's fiction, here becomes a 'diseased participation in other people's consciousness' (ch. 1) which creates only torment.

Latimer's description of his 'preternaturally heightened sense of hearing, making audible to one a roar of sound where others find perfect stillness' (ch. 1) anticipates, as Gillian Beer has noted, a famous *Middlemarch* passage: 'If we had a keen vision and feeling of all ordinary human life, it would be like hearing the grass grow and the squirrel's heart beat, and we should die of that roar which lies on the other side of silence. As it is, the quickest of us walk about well wadded with stupidity.'[27] There has been, however, a complete shift in register. While Latimer quails in horror, the *Middlemarch* version forms a plea to the reader to extend sympathy towards the frequent sufferings of everyday life. Eliot's language draws on the intense excitement generated in contemporary science by the seeming extension of the possibilities of vision offered by microscopic studies. Lewes, for example, speaks in *Sea-side Studies* of our recognition of the 'great drama which is incessantly enacted in every drop of water, on every inch of earth. Then, and only then, do we realise the mighty complexity, the infinite splendour of Nature.'[28] The microscope, he suggests, is not just 'the mere extension of a faculty, it is a new sense'. The scientist with the microscope begins 'where most of us end, with seeing things removed from us – kept distant by ignorance and the still more obscuring screen of familiarity'.[29]

Eliot granted to Latimer that microscopic extension of vision; a new sense which enabled him to sweep away the screens of familiarity and delve below the accepted social surfaces of his companions. In place of Lewes's celebration of the wonders of nature, however, we have a crippling paralysis; a fermenting heap rather than the glorious drama of the waterdrop. In its unrelenting negativity, 'The Lifted Veil' gives voice to doubts that lie behind much of Eliot's fiction. Although her adherence to the doctrine of sympathy never wavers, one can nonetheless trace in her works elements of a Latimer-like sense of disdain for mental pettiness. Dorothea, the heroine of *Middlemarch*, is blessed with short-sightedness: she is able to retain her passionate belief in others and in the values of social integration, precisely because she is blind to the general low tenor of the Middlemarch mind.[30]

In her descriptions of Latimer's 'diseased participation in other people's consciousness', Eliot deftly turns Lewes's physiological psychology against itself, and also against her own art: their mutual quest to pry into the workings of the mind becomes in itself a form of disease. The very extension of sympathy Eliot desires to create becomes an assault both on her narrator's and on her own sense of selfhood.

Science and art

Working side by side in their separate spheres, Eliot and Lewes shared similar goals: to illuminate the workings of the mind and to give guidance for future action. 'The Lifted Veil', however, puts the activities of both art and science into question. As a text, it overturns the boundaries that define our being: life and death shade into one another; past, present and future meld; and inner psychic life is externalized. The divisions between self and other no longer hold. Gender also becomes an arena of problematic identity.[31] The tale was produced by a supposedly male figure, now suspected to be female, who was writing in the persona of a feminized male. Such instability intensifies the self-reflexive qualities of the text. Eliot's anxieties about public performance as a female, about having the audacity to *assume* a listening voice, lie behind her creation of the psychologically damaged Latimer, crippled by insights he neither desires nor is able creatively to transform.

'The Lifted Veil' is one of Eliot's most innovative texts in narrative terms. It possesses all the hallmarks now identified as 'postmodern': there is a breakdown of linear time, and of divisions between selfhood and other, and perhaps most radical of all, of boundaries between states of life and death. Rather than proclaim 'The Lifted Veil' a text in advance of its time, I would suggest we need to revise the rather limited models of nineteenth-century realism advanced in much postmodernist theory. Eliot's text was not unique in its disruption of linear narrative, or its explorations of the unconscious, but rather took a stage further the questioning of narrative conventions that recur across nineteenth-century fiction. (It is no coincidence that Eliot finished reading Sterne's gloriously disruptive novel, *Tristram Shandy* (1759–67), shortly after she completed 'The Lifted Veil'.[32]) One can also find direct parallels for many of Eliot's innovations in the field of nineteenth-century science which was far from the dull, empiricist enterprise that is often portrayed.

Contemporary science was itself questioning many of the physical and epistemological boundaries explored in 'The Lifted Veil'. Lewes had no time for physiologists who held to the notion that a 'vital principle' (the physiological equivalent of theological notions of a soul) animated living beings. Nor did he view organic life as self-contained, but stressed instead the crucial role of interaction with a surrounding environment: 'so far from organic bodies being independent of external circumstances they become more and more dependent on them as their organization becomes higher, so that *organism* and *medium*, are the two correlative ideas of life'.[33] These theories are developed in *The Physiology of Common Life*, with reference both to physical and psychical life, and were adopted by Eliot to define her artistic methodology. As she noted in a famous letter about her historical novel *Romola* (1862–3): 'It is the habit of my imagination to strive after as full a vision of the medium in which a character moves as of the character itself.'[34] In *The Mill on the Floss* Eliot lavished great attention on the forms and traditions of the surrounding social life which defined Maggie's being. The rituals of Dodson life, from jam-making to the ceremonial unveiling of the new hat, are given in loving detail. In 'The Lifted Veil', by contrast, Eliot merely sketches an outline of Latimer's social environment; her centre of focus lies in the physiological and psychological processes involved in this form of absorption and exchange.

The states of life and death, according to Lewes, should no longer be seen as simply integral to an organism, since they are dependent on interaction with a surrounding medium. Life was also a continuous process of *death*, of growth matched by decay.[35] Taking these principles into the domain of feeling, Lewes developed a theory to suggest that consciousness was an attribute to be found right across the body: the brain was only *one* organ of the mind: 'psychical Life has no special centre, any more than the physical Life has one special centre: it belongs to the whole, and animates the whole'.[36] This conclusion, although unusual at the time, merely developed and extended contemporary work in physiological psychology which was exploring the difficulties of distinguishing between feeling and thinking, and of separating the sensations of the body from those of the so-called mind. Latimer could be seen as an extreme case of this form of psychological permeability, where the thoughts and feelings of others are absorbed in the same way that the body takes oxygen from the surrounding air.

Lewes's theories challenged clear demarcations of life and death, and of the integrity of mind and body. In place of a unified thinking principle, Lewes offered a vision of mind as a confluence of many streams of sensation, where the body as a whole is as important as the brain. The implications of such a theory are developed in *Studies in Animal Life*, where he celebrates the wondrous process of 'universal metamorphosis' in which we are all involved: 'Nothing leaves us as it found us. Every man we meet, every book we read, every picture or landscape we see, every word or tone we hear, mingles with our being and modifies it.'[37] Thus an uneducated servant girl can be found during delirium to be muttering Greek she had unwittingly absorbed from an earlier master.[38] The model of life Lewes celebrates here, where all contact with surrounding life modifies our inner sense of selfhood, becomes in 'The Lifted Veil' a definition of hell. Latimer is entirely open to his surrounding medium; he cannot police his boundaries. The thoughts of others enter his mind despite his own wishes. His inner life ceases to be under his control and becomes instead a mere confluence of all the streams of sensation flowing around him.

Latimer's happiest time was in childhood when, significantly, he was blind for a short period. His range of sensations was narrowed down to a sense of total union with his mother as he sat on her knee 'from morning till night' (ch. 1). Time was excluded; 'the curtain of the future' had not yet been lifted, and Latimer existed, briefly, in an eternal present. Such happy union is shattered, however, by the death of his mother, and now the external world breaks on him sharply, in a range of discordant sounds – the thunder of his father's carriage, the gong for dinner, the tramp of soldiers – which cause him to 'sob and tremble'. Like that hero of Romantic sensibility Jean-Jacques Rousseau, he gains some respite at Geneva in the midst of natural grandeur, as he lies in a boat, gazing up at the mountains, and feels once more in the presence of 'cherishing love'. Such receptivity becomes crippling, however, when nature is replaced by man, and the troubling, but pre-linguistic, sounds of childhood are supplanted by an incessant babble of language which invades and distorts his inner being.

The Mill on the Floss

When Eliot completed 'The Lifted Veil' she noted in her diary that she was going to resume her new novel and to rewrite the first two chapters.[39] Both texts explore the relationship between mind and medium, the role of childhood development and the workings of the unconscious mind, and in the rewritten chapters of *The Mill on the Floss* one can trace the immediate impact of the tale.[40] Both works open in a state of dreamy unconsciousness, but in *The Mill* yearning nostalgia for the past replaces the tale's horror of the future. The narrator of the former takes us back to childhood, where the booming of the mill creates 'a great curtain of sound, shutting one out from the world beyond'.[41] Like Latimer on his mother's knee, before the 'curtain of the future' is lifted, Maggie is protected by the booming of the mill from complete immersion in the world outside. The noise which protects Maggie, however, destroys Latimer, as he is penetrated by a 'roar of sound' thrust, uninvited, into his consciousness.

Like Tom Tulliver, Latimer is given precisely the form of education which is least suited to his nature. After an examination by the phrenologist Mr Letherall, he is forced to embark on a scientific education designed to develop his rational faculties and to curb his artistic tendencies.[42] While the practical Tom is made to wrestle with Latin, Latimer has to resort to reading Plutarch on the sly. His nature is forced to grow up 'in an uncongenial medium, which could never foster it into happy, healthy development' (ch. 1). Eliot is not here attacking scientific education, but rather, as she suggests in a passage she cancelled from the book version, advocating that a good education is one 'which adapts itself to intellectual wants and faculties'.[43]

Tom and Maggie and Latimer all suffer from being reared within a restrictive social medium. Eliot links the 'oppressive narrowness' of Tulliver life to the 'dead-tinted, hollow-eyed, angular skeletons of villages on the Rhône' which, in contrast to the historical splendours of the Rhine castles, 'oppress me with the feeling that human life — very much of it — is a narrow, ugly, grovelling existence, which even calamity does not elevate'.[44] The passage recalls the depiction of Prague in Latimer's vision, which unites both the grandeur of the Rhine, and the sterility of the Rhone. Like Latimer himself, the inhabitants of Prague experience no growth, or renewal, but rather a form of death in life, a 'dusty, weary, time-eaten grandeur of a people doomed to live on in the stale repetition of memories' (ch. 1). These people 'worship wearily in the stifling air of the churches, urged by no fear or hope, but compelled by their doom to be ever old and undying, to live on in the rigidity of habit, as they live on in perpetual mid-day, without the repose of night or the new birth of morning'. Religion does not allay mortification, but rather seems to be its principal agent; there is no revivifying hope for a future life which might break the endless cycle of repetition, the utter dominance of the past within the present. Latimer likewise experiences a 'shrivelled death-in-life', locked in a narrative that can have no progression. To his eyes, the real inhabitants of Prague seem to be the blank statues, 'while the busy, trivial men and women, hurrying to and fro, were a swarm of ephemeral visitants infesting it for a day'. The language again recalls Eliot's depiction of life on the Rhone, her 'cruel conviction that the lives these ruins are the traces of were part of a gross sum of obscure vitality, that will be swept into the same oblivion with the generations of ants and beavers'. In *The Mill on the Floss*, however, such negativity is overcome as Eliot ties 'obscure vitality' into the 'onward tendency of human things'. Memory is cast not as the stultifying 'rigidity of habit', but rather as the moral agency of development and renewal. As Maggie demands of Stephen, 'If the past is not to bind us, where can duty lie?'[45] Maggie and her brother Tom are offered in the end a form of resurrection, a redemption through memory, as they return once more in death to the realm of their childhood. Latimer by contrast can only await passively the outcome of a future which is already a sterile part of memory.

In 1858 Eliot had read Dickens's Christmas story 'The Haunted Man',[46] in which Redlaw, a man tormented by memories, is offered the power to cancel remembrance, both in himself and those he encounters. He learns, to his cost, that all social and personal morality is founded on memory. Eliot neatly reverses this story: Latimer's life is ruined by memory, not the recollections of past misdeeds or misfortunes, but rather his memories of the future which take away all sense of hope or possibility in the present.[47]

Prevision

The accuracy of Latimer's prevision of Prague is confirmed when he sees, projected on the pavement, a light in the shape of a star. It has led him not to a vision of Christ and eternal life, however, but to its very opposite. Within the Jewish synagogue, as the 'Book of the Law' is read out, he feels this 'withered remnant' is of a piece with his vision and shows an even further 'shrivelled death-in-life' than its Christian counterpart. In *Daniel Deronda* Eliot was to employ the Jewish religion as evidence of organic continuity in culture: in 'The Lifted Veil' it points only to a life bereft of hope in the future, and stifled by the detritus of the past.

In exploring Latimer's powers of prevision, Eliot draws on contemporary psychological ideas. Mesmerism, of course, had suggested a similar combination of powers to see both into the minds of others and into the future. As Beryl Gray has noted, Eliot had an earlier friendship and correspondence with the champion of phrenology George Combe, who had introduced her to the works on mesmerism of William Gregory, whose patients included a man who had visions of European cities he had not visited.[48] The power of seeing into others' minds had also received popular discussion in the press, particularly the celebrated case of Zschokke, the German writer, who appeared to possess the power, with regard to a few people, 'of knowing when he came near them, not only their present thought, but much of what was in their memory'.[49] A further link with mesmerism lay in Edgar Allan Poe's popular 1845 story, republished in England as a pamphlet, *Mesmerism 'In Articulo Mortis'* (1846), in which a man is mesmerized at the moment of death. He remains in a trance for seven months and when awakened, cries out '*I say to you that I am dead!*', before his whole body crumbles into a liquid mass of 'detestable putrescence'.[50] Although the medium of resurrection is very different, Poe's and Eliot's tales both feature a scientific experiment which gives speech to the dead. Given John Blackwood's opposition to Eliot's story, it is also interesting to note that in the August 1859 issue of *Blackwood's* he published Edward Bulwer-Lytton's story 'The Haunted and the Haunters; or, the House and the Brain,' in which the apparent haunting of a house is traced to a man who, by sheer power of will, is enabled to live through centuries, an 'execrable Image of Life in Death and Death in Life' and to reactivate by mesmeric power past thoughts and deeds.[51]

Strange powers of the mind were the subject of intense popular and scientific debate in the 1850s. By 1859, however, Eliot's scepticism with regard to phrenology and mesmerism had increased, and her interests focused more directly on mainstream psychology which tended to dismiss the claims of seeing into others' minds but not, interestingly, those for prevision. W. B. Carpenter, A. L. Wigan, Henry Holland and Lewes all explored the phenomenon, treating it generally as an interesting example of the instability of memory and perception. Wigan argued, for example, in *The Duality of Mind* that the 'sentiment of pre-existence' was due to the fact that the brain itself was a dual organ: one brain experiences on its own, and then both are subsequently conjoined.[52] The most influential work in this area, however, was that of Henry Holland, pioneer of the notion of 'double consciousness' which he defined as a state where 'the mind passes by alternation from one state to another, each having the perception of external impressions and appropriate trains of thought, but not linked together by the ordinary gradations, or by mutual memory'.[53]

Eliot's treatment of Latimer's 'diseased sensibility' bears strong parallels to Holland's work, for Latimer's presentiments are turned into a form of double consciousness. Despite Latimer's terrifying vision of his relations with Bertha in the future, he is still impelled by desire for her. Latimer turns his dilemma into an open address to the reader:

Are you unable to give me your sympathy – you who read this? Are you unable to imagine this double consciousness at work within me, flowing on like two parallel streams which never mingle their waters and blend into a common hue? Yet you must have known something of the presentiments that spring from an insight at war with passion; and my visions were only like presentiments intensified to horror. You have known the powerlessness of ideas before the might of impulse; and my visions, when once they had passed into memory, were mere ideas – pale shadows that beckoned in vain, while my hand was grasped by the living and the loved. (ch. 1)

Presentiments here become another form of memory, and Latimer's diseased sensibility merely a mirror of our own. Eliot takes her tale out of the frame of the supernatural in order to highlight the fact that we all suffer from a similar form of double consciousness in our inability to make our actions and desires conform to our rational insights into future possibilities.

The language of the passage, with its reference to flowing streams, draws on the physiological psychology of Holland and Lewes which depicted the mind's processes in terms of streams or channels of sensation. Eliot carefully grounds Latimer's extraordinary mental life within the terms of contemporary science. His first vision conforms to Lewes's depiction of hallucination, in which sensations are excited internally while the mind disregards the evidence of the external senses:[54] Latimer is not asleep for he is aware of his father leaving the room and Pierre entering. Similarly, in accordance with Lewes's theories of perception and the mental channelling of sensation, Bertha's mind remains closed to Latimer due to the intensity of his attention which directs all the 'fluctuations of hope and fear' into 'this one channel' (ch. 1).[55] On his father's death, Latimer's obsessive preoccupation is relaxed and the veil withdrawn.[56] Latimer uses the rigour of a scientist in his attempts to diagnose his complaint: he wonders whether his vision is due to some change in his organization wrought by his illness, which had 'given a firmer tension to my nerves [or] carried off some dull obstruction'. Or whether it was 'a sort of intermittent delirium, concentrating my energy of brain into moments of unhealthy activity'. Given the precision of these analyses, his assertion that he is forced to accept the validity of his prevision, since it is proved to have a 'fixed relation' to the incalculable processes of others' minds, carries with it a degree of scientific authority.

In her ability to withstand Latimer's intrusive powers, Bertha plays a similar role to the savage street child in Dickens's 'Haunted Man' who alone resists Redlaw's powers to destroy memory. Like the urchin, Bertha lacks the customary attributes of humanity, possessing a mind that is at once narrower and meaner than those of her peers. In creating this figure who, of course, is seen only through Latimer's eyes, Eliot was constructing a character type that she would return to again and again. As a form of 'Water-Nixie' Bertha is connected to the self-absorbed Rosamond Vincy in *Middlemarch*, and even more directly to the 'Nereid', Gwendolen Harleth, in *Daniel Deronda* whom we first meet dressed in 'sea-green robes' as 'a sort of serpent'.[57] This image reprises that of Bertha, who was similarly dressed in 'green weeds', and who later appears in Latimer's agonized prevision with a 'great emerald brooch on her bosom, a studded serpent with diamond eyes' (ch. 1). In many ways *Daniel Deronda* is a rewriting of 'The Lifted Veil', a counteracting of its claustrophobic, pessimistic vision. The withered 'death-in-life' of the Jewish synagogue becomes a vital, organic inheritance, and the powers of prevision accorded to Mordecai become a powerfully enabling force.[58] The demonic Bertha is rewritten as Gwendolen whose narrow self-absorption becomes the sympathetic centre of the book. 'Could there be', the narrator demands, 'a slenderer, more insignificant thread in human history than this consciousness of a girl, busy with her small inferences of the way in which she could make her life pleasant?' The answer amounts to a complete refutation of Latimer's perspective on life:

What in the midst of that mighty drama are girls and their blind visions? They are the Yea or Nay of that good for which men are enduring and fighting. In these delicate vessels is borne onward through the ages the treasure of human affections.[59]

Far from standing outside the moral pale, the figure of Bertha in this later text comes to embody the very essence of humanity.

Resurrection

Following his marriage to Bertha, Latimer loses his only outlet for anticipation and desire: under the pressure of emotion provoked by his father's death, he sees, finally, through the 'blank prosaic wall' of Bertha's mind, uncovering all its pettiness and cruelty (ch. 2). With its silent alienation and repulsion, their marriage traces a pattern to be followed by Gwendolen and Grandcourt, where polite phrases hide the violence of undisclosed desires.[60] Hope is briefly revived for Latimer with the expectation of his friend Charles Meunier's visit. He feels that Meunier's presence 'would be to me like a transient resurrection into a happier pre-existence'. Yet his desire is met not by spiritual fulfilment but by grotesque parody. 'Transient resurrection' receives literal, physiological enactment in Meunier's blood transfusion into the corpse of Bertha's maid, Mrs Archer.

Eliot's refusal to accept the judgement of her publisher to cut this scene suggests how firmly it was embedded within her conception of the tale as a whole. Like Lewes, who was at this time heavily involved in vivisection and biological experimentation, she too was trying to disentangle the material secrets of life and death. Eliot had accompanied Lewes to Munich and Dresden in 1858 where he met, and worked with, some of the greatest chemists and physiologists of the era.[61] On his return he was possessed with what he terms in *Sea-side Studies* a 'nervous fever', sacrificing every animal he could in his pursuit of the secrets of the ganglia.[62] Small boys were employed to keep up a continuous supply of live frogs. In his two articles on the blood in *Blackwood's* in 1858, he describes in graphic detail his various experiments on the triton (or newt), where circulation continued in the tail after the removal of the heart. Irritability and all the vital properties were preserved several hours after the heart had ceased to beat. Nor could the condition of the heart itself be taken as a measure of death. Lewes cites various gory anecdotes to illustrate the fact that the heart can keep on beating even after death: one woman's heart had rhythmic movements twenty-seven hours after she had been guillotined.[63] Lewes goes on to describe his own experiments which have shown that the heart continues to beat even after it has been removed from the body; if it is cut in two, the two halves will continue to beat separately.[64]

Such experiments, Lewes suggests, create in the mind of the anatomist a 'tremulous awe': 'The beating of the heart, which from his childhood he has learned to associate in some mysterious manner with life and emotion, he here sees occurring under circumstances removed from all possible suggestions of emotion or life. What mean those throbbings?'[65] This quest for meaning in a materialist universe pulses through 'The Lifted Veil', where the higher aspirations of the soul seem to become merely the diseased effects of a 'morbid organization'. While the beating of the heart suggests the possibility of physical life after death, Latimer experiences a form of spiritual death in life. In Lewes's model of the human organism, the soul, that sacrosanct principle of theology, became a mere description of the nervous sensibility which traversed the entire body. Lewes challenged his offended readers to offer a better explanation: 'It is a topic on which no man will wisely dogmatise. The veil of mystery will never be lifted. We who stand before that veil, and speculate as to what is behind it, can but build systems; we cannot see the truth.'[66] Eliot's attempt to lift the veil is framed, in this instance, by a negativity which never creeps into Lewes's works, where the excitement of discovery keeps at bay more troubling metaphysical speculation.

As Kate Flint has shown, Eliot was drawing in the transfusion scene on the contemporary work on blood transfusions of E. Brown-Séquard, himself a possible model for Meunier.[67] In his first article on blood, Lewes describes Brown-Séquard's transfusions of a rabbit, and refers the 'curious reader' to Brown-Séquard's *Journal de la Physiologie* for further details of other experiments.[68] Eliot here takes up that role of curious reader, developing contemporary speculation as to the possibility of reawakening human life. Her vision of resurrected life, however, is more disturbing than the details of the experiment itself. Mrs Archer comes to life only to give vent to her hatred of Bertha, and to extract her revenge. Latimer, for the first and only time, invokes God, thereby heavily underscoring the entire absence of any sense of spiritual afterlife in the text:

Great God! Is this what it is to live again ... to wake up with our unstilled thirst upon us, with our unuttered curses rising to our lips, with our muscles ready to act out their half-committed sins? (ch. 2)

As Lewes remarked: 'What mean those throbbings?' The division between life and death has been severed, but only to produce a terrifyingly precise, physiological vision of the afterlife. As in Lewes's vivisected specimens, the irritability of the muscles remains after death. Blood, Lewes noted, contains our past, present and future.[69] The transfusion, in Eliot's tale, turns the potentiality of the future into a mere function of physiology.

As the thoughts of others penetrated Latimer's consciousness against his will, so Meunier's blood penetrates Mrs Archer's body without her control, in a classic embodiment of male science dominating female nature.[70] Eliot here takes Lewes's theory that selfhood, or identity, is the product of interchange between organism and medium to its ultimate conclusion: even in death we are not inviolable. The extraordinary gender dynamics of the scene represent a culmination of the general misogyny of the text. Bertha is revealed for what she is, a scheming potential murderess, and a woman enters the afterlife George Eliot so yearned to achieve through her art. Mrs Archer attains this desired state only through male agency, however, and its tenor is despicable. Latimer's role in this scene departs, crucially, from his usual passivity. While Meunier supplies the blood, Latimer supplies the air which enables Mrs Archer to give voice once more.[71] In the most intimate physical action in the text, he breathes life into her corpse.[72] The consequences of this action are ambiguous, for Mrs Archer's utterance functions primarily not as a revelation of truth, and hence a vehicle for justice, but rather as a statement of hatred for another woman. The scene itself is notoriously difficult to read.[73] Undoubtedly there are levels of self-doubt, even hatred, operating here as Eliot struggles with the gender politics of her own bid for authorship. Yet it is important to remember that 'The Lifted Veil' is designedly an autobiography of a *perverted* mind that interprets all visions and events through the narrow lens of timid egotism.

Following the loss of her religious faith, Eliot sought the courage to '*do without opium*', and to create her own afterlife through art. In 'The Lifted Veil', as in *Middlemarch*, she constructs a scientific analogue of her own narrative practice. While *Middlemarch* is to offer us an heroic vision of science, as a work of the imagination which illumines the outer darkness, science in 'The Lifted Veil', by contrast, functions on an unrelentingly physical plane. Vision and insight become mere functions of a disordered brain, and resurrection a quirk of physiology. Although Meunier, the physician, is the most humane figure in the text, he creates merely a spurious form of life which gives vent only to curses and 'half-committed sins'. For Latimer, the resurrection scene is 'of one texture with the rest of my existence' (ch. 2) where life is defined by death, insight is a form of curse, and creativity leads only to a form of paralysis.

'The Lifted Veil' had its own curious form of afterlife.[74] Eliot suggested including it, together with 'Brother Jacob', in a cheap edition of her novels planned by Blackwood in 1866. He returned both stories, advising against inclusion: 'They are both as clever as can be, but there is a painful want of light about them.'[75] In 1873 Blackwood changed his mind and asked if he could include 'The Lifted Veil' in a collection of 'Tales from *Blackwood's*'. This time Eliot refused, noting that she still cared 'for the idea it embodies and which justifies its painfulness' but that she would not want to 'send it forth in its dismal loneliness'.[76] She enclosed, however, a motto to accompany future publication:

Give me no light, great Heaven, but such as turns
To energy of human fellowship;
No powers beyond the growing heritage
That makes completer manhood.

It seems, ostensibly, to fit the entire tale within a neat moral framework, yet its personal form further extends the troubling identification of Eliot and her narrator, while the appeal to 'great Heaven', echoing Latimer's 'Great God', only underscores the absence of such a power either in the tale or in Eliot's humanist philosophy.[77] The troubling ambivalences of the tale cannot be so easily contained. The motto looks forward, however, to *Daniel Deronda*, which reworks so many of the themes of 'The Lifted Veil', cancelling its misogyny, and setting Gwendolen's paralysing powers of prevision against the 'forecasting ardour' of Mordecai,[78] whose imaginative power blended past, present and future into a creative whole.

'Brother Jacob'

'Brother Jacob', Eliot's only other story, was written in 1860 on her return from the trip to Italy which marked her completion of *The Mill on the Floss*. As with 'The Lifted Veil', she speaks of it in rather disparaging terms, describing it in her diary as 'a slight tale'.[79] It was similarly composed at a time when she was once again depressed and questioning her creative powers.[80] Like its predecessor, it can also be read as a meditation on the powers of authorship, and a questioning of many of the moral values which structure her other works.

While writing 'The Lifted Veil' Eliot had read Swift's 'Tale of a Tub' (1704), with its famous digression on madness. All forms of human unveiling or dissection are to be avoided, Swift suggests in his playfully sardonic tone, for they only expose further layers of human weakness.[81] Rather than pursuing the science of exposure, we should content ourselves with the 'superficies of things', and rest happy in the felicity of being 'well deceived'.[82] 'Brother Jacob' is a tale about deception. Where 'The Lifted Veil' pursues the darker side of Swift's vision, 'Brother Jacob' adopts his satiric mode. The tale is a fable, as the epigraph from La Fontaine, warning readers about deceivers, suggests.

Its mocking, satirical tone, however, is closer to La Fontaine than to Swift or Pope. As with 'The Lifted Veil', such a radical shift in literary style has caused problems for critics and readers who turn to the story expecting a replication of the warm humanism expressed in the novels. The story is undoubtedly moral, and indeed pointedly tells us so throughout, but evinces no sympathetic concern for the objects of its satire, neither the anti-hero David Faux, nor his brother, the childlike 'idiot', Jacob.[83]

While travelling in Italy, Eliot wrote to John Blackwood that seeing such great art threw her into a state of 'humiliating passivity', finding her own art 'dwarfed by comparison' such that 'I should never have courage for more creation of my own'. She is cheered, however, by 'the comparative rarity even here of great and truthful art, and the abundance of wretched imitation and falsity'.[84] David Faux, the central protagonist of 'Brother Jacob', is the epitome, as his name suggests, of falsity. Not only does he lie and deceive, as he makes off with his mother's guineas, he also adopts the profession of confectioner, spinning sugar into more and more elaborate creations, of little substance, but 100% profit. If he had lived, the narrator observes, in 'present times, and enjoyed the advantages of a Mechanics' Institute, he would certainly have taken to literature and have written reviews' (ch. 1).

If Latimer is a failed author, paralysed by too much insight and lack of trust in a receiving audience, David Faux is a form of a commercially successful one, who trades in 'superficies' and enticing appearances. We are here in the territory of Eliot's essay 'Silly Novels by Lady Novelists' (1856) where she castigated members of the 'mind-and-millinery school' of writing, who 'lack an appreciation of the sacredness of the writer's art' and in place of works of imaginative power produce instead literary 'sweetmeats'.[85] Continuing the culinary analogy, Eliot suggested that 'Society is a very culpable entity, and has to answer for the manufacture of many unwholesome commodities, from bad pickles to bad poetry.' She was particularly concerned with the response to female writers, where journalistic appreciation was at 'boiling pitch' when 'a woman's talent is at zero . . . and if ever she reaches excellence, critical enthusiasm drops to the freezing point'.[86]

This was of course written before the launch of Eliot's own career in fiction, but one can see here the same anxieties about authorship and literary consumption which underpin 'Brother Jacob'. David Faux's resurrection as a successful confectioner is made possible by his credulous audience who accept his false tales of his wealthy uncle and his life in the West Indies, because it suits their self-interest to do so. The denizens of Grimworth consume his stories as avidly as they do his cakes. Society gets the literature it deserves. Even great literature is perverted by the receiving mind so that it is made to pander to a debased taste: thus Mrs Steene, the vet's wife, knew many passages of Byron by heart, 'which had given her a distaste for domestic occupations' (ch. 2). Similarly, David Faux himself had 'bought the story of "Inkle and Yarico"' (ch. 1) which features the unpleasant exploitation of the beautiful Native American woman, Yarico, by the young English adventurer Thomas Inkle who sets out for the West Indies to make his fortune. On landing in America to search for provisions, all his shipmates are murdered by Native Americans, but Inkle is saved by Princess Yarico who hides him for several months. They learn each other's languages, and he makes great promises to her about their future life in England. They are rescued and taken to Barbados, where the 'prudent and frugal' Inkle sells Yarico as a slave, merely raising her price when she informs him that she is pregnant. David Faux's literary judgement is of a piece with the rest of his behaviour: he feels 'very sorry for poor Mr Inkle'. Eliot pointedly notes that this response suggests 'his ideas might not have been below a certain mark of the literary calling'. With his odious 'self-complacency', narrow self-interest and utter lack of any emotional sensitivity, David Faux is linked to the band of talentless writers and critics attacked in 'Silly Novels'.

The story of Inkle and Yarico, which was first published by Richard Steele in the *Spectator* (13 March 1711), plays a crucial role in Eliot's story, at both a symbolic and thematic level. The original context of Steele's story is of significance.[87] The piece starts with a 'Common-Place Talker' who insults a lady of 'Taste and Understanding' by repeating a scurrilous tale of female frailty and appetite.[88] She responds by noting that 'You Men are Writers, and can represent us Women as unbecoming as you please in your Works, while we are unable to return the Injury.' Her tale of 'Inkle and Yarico' is her attempt to correct centuries of literary inequality. Steele responds with tears in his eyes: David Faux, by contrast, compounds the injuries done to women by sympathizing with Inkle. He follows the pattern set by critics who fail to respond to the greatness of a Mrs Gaskell or Currer

Bell (Charlotte Brontë), and instead fall for the imitative froth of weak writers.[89]

In both 'Brother Jacob' and Steele's story, the tale of 'Inkle and Yarico' is symbolically embedded within an overarching concern with literary taste and judgement, and the woman writer's role within the marketplace. Eliot's anger against the critics who rounded on her once her identity was revealed, and the whole industry revolving around the imposter Joseph Liggins, who had claimed to be the author of her works, is vested in her contemptuous portrait of David Faux.[90]

The thematic parallels with 'Inkle and Yarico' are also strong. Inkle had been educated by his father into 'an early Love of Gain . . . giving him a quick View of Loss and Advantage, and preventing the natural Impulses of his Passions, by Prepossession towards his Interests'.[91] These characteristics are replicated in David Faux who was 'a young man greatly given to calculate consequences' (ch. 1), such that he seems to have no natural feelings at all; his loving mother is nothing other than a quick source of money for him. The harsh laws of nineteenth-century laissez-faire economics, with their elevation of self-interest to a principle of all social virtue, are here refracted back through the earlier critique of capitalist greed.[92] David Faux's dreams are culled from 'Inkle and Yarico': he sails to the West Indies in response to the story, expecting to find a princess who would load him with jewels (and could then be discarded afterwards), and a black population who would bow to his innate superiority. His debased literary responses form part of his social dreams of exploitation. His fantasies of having a woman serve him as a slave take on an urgent political resonance as he sails towards the slave economy which lay at the heart of the British colonial empire.[93]

Fortunately, Faux is not granted a Yarico, nor does his white skin guarantee him a place of pre-eminence in Jamaican society. He is reduced, instead, to working in kitchens. Eliot does not portray directly his life there, but her attitude to this slave-owning economy is clearly imprinted on her satirical portrait of Mrs Chaloner, the rector's wife, whose grandfather had owned sugar plantations. She finds the confectioner a man of principle and discernment because he reassures her that 'the missionaries were the only cause of the negro's discontent' (ch. 2). Guilt, with reference to slave labour, or the consumption of illicitly purchased cakes, can easily be assuaged. Although David Faux does not participate directly in the triangular slave trade, in his adopted guise of Edward Freely, confectioner, he turns the sugar produced by slave labour into tarts, etc., generating 100% profit for himself. In a reversal of his early magic trick performed for his idiot brother Jacob, he turns sugar into gold.

Parallels with Silas Marner

As with 'The Lifted Veil', 'Brother Jacob' is engaged in direct dialogue with its parallel novel, in this case *Silas Marner*. Both tale and novel are concerned with the workings of greed and of memory, and the processes of social development. Both have at their heart the theft of gold. Silas is robbed twice, once by his fellow brother in the Lantern Yard religious community, William Dane, who frames him for monetary theft and thus robs him of his reputation, and once by Dunstan Cass who steals his cherished guineas. Like David Faux, who similarly employs blackmail, Dunstan is the epitome of selfishness, convinced that the rest of the world is only there to be exploited for his own advantage. The robbery and the gold fulfil rather different functions in the two texts, however. David's robbery is carefully planned, but comically presented, as his attempt to bury his ill-gotten gains is disrupted by the appearance of his pitchfork-waving brother who is to prove, six years later, his nemesis. Dunstan's robbery is unplanned, dramatically presented and followed by an immediate nemesis as he tumbles into the stone-pit. David tries to trick his brother into believing that the guineas, if buried, will transform into the far more desirable shape of yellow lozenges. *Silas Marner* rewrites this cynical manipulation into a humanist miracle of transformation. Silas loses his guineas, but he finds in their place something of far greater value: the soft golden curls of Eppie, the child who is to draw him back, through love, into a social community once more. Eliot prefaced the novel with an epigraph from William Wordsworth's 'Michael' (1800):

> a child, more than all other gifts
> That earth can offer to declining man,
> Brings hope with it, and forward-looking thoughts.

Silas Marner is the very opposite of 'The Lifted Veil', opening up the future, which Latimer could only dread, as a place of hope and possibility.

While *Silas Marner* endorses Wordsworthian values of memory and community, 'Brother Jacob' addresses similar issues, to very different effect. We have in the tale very familiar Wordsworthian themes: a boy who forsakes his loving family (including an idiot brother) and country home to better himself and goes to the bad. It possesses neither the elegiac qualities of 'Michael', however, nor the affectionate concern of Wordsworth's 'The Idiot Boy' (1798), and, as with 'The Lifted Veil', it puts into question the moral power of memory. While Latimer's distorted powers of vision takes away any solace from the past, or hope for the future, collapsing present and future into undifferentiated time, the idiot Jacob lives in an eternal present, with no real distinctions between past and present. When he bursts into his brother's shop yelling 'b'other Zavy' and demanding 'mother's zinnies' from the lozenge jar (ch. 3), it is as if the intervening years have never happened. Brother Davy, guineas and lozenges are locked in his mind in an unbreakable link. Memory does not beautify the present by linking it through affection with the past. Jacob's mind operates to obliterate time and perspective, and his affection is shown to be based purely on physical greed. There is no escape for David: Jacob would always keep returning to his shop, 'like a wasp to the honey-pot' (ch. 3). Cunning is contrasted with innocence and both are found to be distasteful. Jacob's limited animal intelligence highlights the equally limiting selfishness of his brother.

'The Idiot Brother'

'The Idiot Brother', one of Eliot's working titles for the tale, stresses her interest in the fact of Jacob's idiocy. We do not know why the title was changed: possibly because it made the subject matter unappealing, or because it raised expectations of a Wordsworthian treatment which would not be fulfilled. Eliot is not concerned with the mysterious otherness of her creation, nor is he a sympathetic figure. With his huge frame, ever-present pitchfork and insatiable appetite for dumplings and lozenges, he is rather a figure of fun. Eliot was writing at a point in English history when, for the very first time, specialist asylums were being built to house and treat idiots, and hope was held out for their educability.[94] Eliot does not pursue this line of thought, however, for her interest lies elsewhere: in the physiological workings of a mind which lay outside the normal networks of connection. (This element, too, was to be carried forward to *Silas Marner* in Silas's fits of catalepsy which disrupt his sense of memory and temporality.) Jacob wrecks his brother's plans for he possesses a mind that lies outside normal calculation: 'David, not having studied the psychology of idiots, was not aware that they are not to be wrought upon by imaginative fears . . . It's of no use to have foresight when you are dealing with an idiot: he is not to be calculated upon' (ch. 1). Stratagems are useless against a mind that does not have a sense of future possibility, and can be swayed by every passing sensation. Jacob, in the language of nineteenth-century evolutionary theory, is a throwback, or survival, an exemplum of a more primitive mindset. He has a later, very interesting parallel in *Daniel Deronda* in that archetype of civilized violence, Grandcourt, who, despite his urbane sophistication, is none the less constantly compared to reptiles and creatures on the bottom of the evolutionary scale. He too possesses a mind which cannot be calculated upon.[95] In the words of G. H. Lewes's 1861 essay 'Uncivilised Man': 'Many of the things noticeable as characteristic of the savage are found lingering amongst ourselves.'[96]

Jacob takes his place in the broader contemplation of social and psychological development which runs through the narrative. Eliot was writing at a time when Charles Darwin's *Origin of Species* (published November 1859), was being hotly debated, and her friend Herbert Spencer's theories of universal progression from simplicity to complexity were setting the agenda of social and psychological discussion.[97] At the heart of Spencer's theory was the belief that the mind, like the social organism, evolved to an ever-increasing level of complexity; the economic theory of the division of labour became a universal principle. There was a homologous relation, he suggested in his 1860 essay 'The social organism' between the circulation of 'the blood in a living body and the consumable and circulating commodities in the body-politic'.[98] Eliot's fiction follows this trajectory, moving from a consideration of the circulation of the blood in 'The Lifted Veil' to that of the circulation of commodities in 'Brother Jacob'. But she is far from sharing Spencer's sanguine sense of necessary and unending progression.

David, in opening his confectioner's shop, is taking over labour formerly conducted in the home, and thus adding another layer of complexity to social organization. Eliot comments archly, 'I am not ignorant that this sort of thing is called the inevitable course of civilisation, division of labour, and so forth' (ch. 2).[99] Yet what if the matrons of Grimworth cannot employ their time, thus released, in any better way, and the production of 'leathery' pastry was in fact the very height of their possible attainments? Thus the 'progress of civilisation' in Grimworth 'was not otherwise apparent than in the impoverishment of men, the gossiping idleness of women, and the heightening prosperity of Mr Edward Freely'. Under the comedy there is a serious point: Eliot is attacking models of social progress which have at their heart economic theories of self-interest. What is good for Edward Freely is not necessarily of benefit to the social organism as a whole.

In Eliot's view, social progression had to be founded on moral advancement. She shared with Lewes a critical response to H. T. Buckle's *History of Civilization in England* (1857–61) which was the subject of intense debate at that time: Buckle attributed the rise of civilization entirely to rational calculation, without giving any allowance either for the development of inherited qualities or the growth of moral powers.[100] Eliot cautiously endorsed ideas of social progress, but with a strong sense that we are never as advanced as we think. Thus Maggie, in *The Mill on the Floss*, beats her fetish, and the citizens of St Ogg's exhibit 'a variation of Protestantism unknown to Bossuet': 'their moral notions, although held with strong tenacity, seem to have no standard beyond hereditary custom'.[101] This worship of hereditary custom is clearly exhibited in Grimworth, where families held it 'a point of honour . . . to buy their sugar and their flannel at the shops where their fathers and mothers had bought before them' (ch. 2), while the historical regression to fetishism is evident in Jacob's vision of his brother as 'a sort of sweet-tasted fetish' (ch. 1) – a form of fetishism to be re-enacted in *Silas Marner* in Silas's worship of his gold.

We should not, Eliot suggests, take our evaluation of our place within civilization too seriously. David Faux, for all his belief in his advanced attainments, is no better than his brother Jacob, who, as an idiot, was placed on the lowest rung of the human evolutionary scale. Both brothers are mere creatures of greed, and both stand outside the realm of morality.

David successfully remakes himself as a confectioner, Edward Freely, and, like his commodities, 'made his way gradually into Grimworth homes . . . in spite of some initial repugnance' (ch. 2). He is just about to form a successful match with a wealthy young lady of the town, when Jacob rushes into his shop, claims kinship and starts to devour everything in sight. David is forced, stumblingly, into his only moral utterance of the book, as he attempts to evade detection: 'All men are our brothers, and idiots particular so' (ch. 3). David has, unwittingly, seized on the anti-slavery slogan 'Am I not a man and a brother?', which had become, in the hands of the satirical magazine *Punch*, a source of repeated cartoons on our relations to oppressed peoples.[102] For the reader, if not for David, the moral is clear: as a form of life he indeed stands lower than the slaves he had hoped to dominate in the West Indies, or his idiot brother whose kinship he has sought so desperately to deny. Brotherhood is a concept he has utterly failed to grasp at any level – physiological, social or moral.

In *Adam Bede* an uncharacteristically harsh satiric note crept into the narrative as Eliot unveiled our social hypocrisy: should a wealthy young man 'happen to spoil a woman's existence for her, [he] will make it up with expensive *bon-bons*, packed up and directed by his own hand'.[103] That novel challenged such an unequal exchange, where sweets could be used to offset human lives. Arthur Donnithorne has to learn the hard way that 'Our deeds carry their terrible consequences . . . consequences that are hardly ever confined to ourselves.'[104] David Faux has similarly to learn that all actions have consequences. The moral is pointedly delivered at the end:

Here ends the story of Mr David Faux, confectioner, and his brother Jacob. And we see in it, I think, an admirable instance of the unexpected forms in which the great Nemesis hides herself.

Jacob is like a comic form of Raffles, who in *Middlemarch* exposes deeds Bulstrode had thought were long dead and buried. Burial, however, will not turn guineas into lozenges, nor vice into virtue.

Although the moral teaching of the tale follows that of Eliot's other works, its effects are very different. The fabular form, unlike the realist novel, has no concern with character development or change. We do not witness any moral growth on David's part, nor dawning recognition of immoral behaviour. He is almost defined, like Jacob, by his non-educability. David, no doubt, will move to yet another town and attempt, unsuccessfully, to reinvent himself again. The engrafting of the concerns of moral realism on to a fable produces, in a peculiar twist, a moral structure which swings dangerously close to the paradigms of self-interested calculation that the tale itself attacks: avoid wrongdoing because you are bound to get caught.

In returning Eliot's manuscript of 'The Lifted Veil' Blackwood had tried to soften the blow of his rejection. Others, he suggests, are perhaps 'not so fond of sweets as I am'.[105] Is this harsh satirical tale of a confectioner Eliot's response? Both tales address similar issues to the novels, in their concerns with writing, and the structures of mind, memory and history, yet they adopt different generic forms: Gothic horror, fable and eighteenth-century satire. In the tension thus generated between form and content lies their strength and their challenge.

Notes

1. *Journals*, p. 77. Eliot had finished *Adam Bede* on 16 November 1858, and corrected the last proof sheets on 15 January 1859. We know that she had immediately started planning *The Mill on the Floss* since she went into London on 12 January to consult the Annual Register 'for cases of *inundation*' (*Journals*, p. 76). Eliot and George Henry Lewes moved from Richmond to Wimbledon on 11 February 1859. 'The Lifted Veil' was probably begun between 15 January and 11 February 1859.

2. *Letters*, III, 41.

3. Eliot had desired that the policy of anonymous publication adhered to by *Blackwood's Edinburgh Magazine* should be broken in this case in order that the story be published under the name of George Eliot. Lewes wrote to Blackwood on 13 June 1859, suggesting this course of action, as it would help to quash rumours that Joseph Liggins was the author of her previous works (*Letters*, III, 83): see note 90.

4. Blackwood wrote to his brother William on 15 June 1859: 'I daresay I am the only editor who would have objected to the name in the present furor. I suppose the other Magazines would give any money for a scrap with George Eliot's name attached' (*Letters*, III, 112 n. 6).

5. *Letters*, III, 67; John Blackwood to George Eliot, 18 May 1859.

6. *Essays*, p. 271. See also *Adam Bede*, ch. 17 for a similar statement of artistic purpose. In both Eliot insists that art should extend our sympathies to the

common man, with all his faults, rather than towards false, idealized characters.

7. *Letters*, III, 111; 5 July 1859.

8. *Letters*, II, 377; to Sara Hennell, 19 August 1857.

9. *Letters*, III, 67.

10. See J. W. Cross, *George Eliot's Life as Related in Her Letters and Journals*, 3 vols. (William Blackwood: Edinburgh and London, 1885). The journal commenced in Geneva in 1849, and Cross removed the section up to Eliot's voyage with Lewes to Antwerp in July 1854.

11. *Letters*, I, 335. Eliot also wrote to her half-sister, Fanny, on 30 March 1850: 'I am sad at the sight of my own country and feel more of an outcast here than at Geneva' (*Letters*, I, 333; to Mrs Henry Houghton).

12. *Letters*, III, 124; to Blackwood, 30 July 1859. Eliot and Lewes's close friend Herbert Spencer, the philosopher, had been let in on the secret, but had then betrayed it to the publisher John Chapman. Jealousy of her publishing success seemed to lie beind Spencer's increasing hostility to Eliot at this time: see Gordon S. Haight, *George Eliot: A Biography* (Oxford: Oxford University Press, 1968), p. 292. Blackwood linked the darkness of the tale directly to Eliot's sense of betrayal: he wished 'the author in a happier frame of mind and not thinking of unsympathising untrustworthy keepers of secrets' (*Letters*, III, 112; 8 July 1859). Eliot responded in similar terms when she wrote to Blackwood thanking him for his gift of a dog: 'Pug is come! – come to fill up the void left by false and narrow-hearted friends. I see already that he is without envy, hatred, or malice – that he will betray no secrets, and feel neither pain at my success nor pleasure in my chagrin' (*Letters*, III, 124; 30 July 1859).

13. *Letters*, III, 38.

14. *Letters*, II, 416.

15. *Letters*, III, 66; 6 May 1859.

16. *Letters*, III, 366: Eliot wrote to Barbara Bodichon on 26 December 1860 that she had

faith in the working-out of higher possibilities than the Catholic or any other church has presented, and those who have strength to wait and endure, are bound to accept no formula which their whole souls – their intellect as well as their emotions – do not embrace with entire reverence. The highest 'calling and election' is to *do without opium* and live through all our pain with conscious, clear-eyed endurance.

17. *Letters*, III, 170; 3? October? 1859. Eliot wrote to Cara Bray: 'The weight of my future life – the self-questioning whether my nature will be able to meet the heavy demands upon it, both of personal duty and intellectual production, presses upon me almost continually in a way that prevents me even from tasting the quiet joy I might have in the *work done*.'

18. *Letters* III, 95–6; Sara Hennell to George Eliot, 26 June 1859. Eliot had been

contemplating this work while she was in Geneva and on her return, the timing thus coinciding with the chronological conclusion of 'The Lifted Veil'.

19. G. H. Lewes, *The Biographical History of Philosophy*, revised edn (London: John Parker, 1857), p. xv.

20. G. H. Lewes, *Comte's Philosophy of the Sciences* (London: Bohn, 1853), p. 41.

21. Adytum is the most sacred part of a church.

22. Although these views are, of course, voiced by the narrator, Latimer, they bear a strong similarity to Eliot's own reflections voiced elsewhere. As with nearly all first-person narratives, the boundaries between authorial and narrating voice often blur.

23. In what has come to be known as the 'paradox of the fortunate fall', Adam and Eve in *Paradise Lost* (1671) are promised 'A Paradise within thee, happier far' (XII, 586–7), when they leave the unchanging world of Eden. (This passage was marked by Eliot in her copy, now held in Dr Williams's Library, London. See William Baker, *The George Eliot–George Henry Lewes Library: An Annotated Catalogue of their Books at Dr Williams's Library, London* (London, 1977).) Knowledge and death are the twin consequences of Eve's consumption of the apple.

24. George Eliot, *The Legend of Jubal and Other Poems, Old and New*, Cabinet edition (Edinburgh and London: William Blackwood, 1878–80), p. 8.

25. Ibid., p. 42.

26. Her poem 'Armgart' (1870), for example, features a singer who loses her voice, a scenario that is replicated in *Daniel Deronda* (1876) in the representation of the Princess.

27. Gillian Beer, 'Myth and the single consciousness: *Middlemarch* and *The Lifted Veil*', in Ian Adam (ed.), *This Particular Web: Essays on Middlemarch* (Toronto: Toronto University Press, 1975), p. 99. George Eliot, *Middlemarch*, 3 vols., Cabinet edition (Edinburgh and London: William Blackwood, 1878–80), Bk. 2, ch. 20.

28. G. H. Lewes, *Sea-side Studies* (Edinburgh and London: William Blackwood, 1858), p. 55.

29. Ibid.

30. Eliot allows Dorothea to move away from Middlemarch at the end of the novel. Her ideals do not have to be compromised by too close an acquaintance with Middlemarch residents.

31. For an exploration of some of these issues, see Sandra M. Gilbert and Susan Gubar, *The Madwoman in the Attic: The Woman Writer and the Nineteenth-Century Literary Imagination* (New Haven: Yale University Press, 1979), pp. 443–77.

32. Entry of 31 May 1859, *Lewes Ms Journal*.

33. Lewes, *Comte's Philosophy of the Sciences*, p. 167.

34. *Letters*, IV, 96–7; to R. H. Hutton, 8 August 1863. Eliot continues: 'The psychological causes which prompted me to give such details of Florentine

life and history as I have given, are precisely the same as those which determined me in giving the details of English village life in *Silas Marner* [1861], or the "Dodson" life, out of which were developed the destinies of poor Tom and Maggie [in *The Mill on the Floss* (1860)].'

35. The application of cell theory to animal life by Theodor Schwann in 1839 had revolutionized biological understanding: each cell had a life independent of the whole, and the life of the whole thus contained a continuous process of death, as cells were continually dying and being replaced. See G. H. Lewes, *The Physiology of Common Life* (Edinburgh and London: William Blackwood, 1859), II, 424–8.

36. Lewes, The Physiology of Common Life, II, 5.

37. G. H. Lewes, *Studies in Animal Life* (London: Smith Elder, 1862), p. 78.

38. This example had been discussed by Coleridge in *Biographia Literaria* (1817) and became standard in nineteenth-century discussions of the movements of the unconscious mind, both in popular and medical texts. See Jenny Bourne Taylor and Sally Shuttleworth (eds.), *Embodied Selves: An Anthology of Psychological Texts, 1830–1890* (Oxford: Oxford University Press, 1998), pp. 67–76.

39. Entry of 27 April 1859, *Journals*, p. 77.

40. Chapter 1 depicts the narrator's dreaming reverie about the Mill, and chapter 2 opens the narrative action with a discussion among the Tullivers about Tom's education.

41. George Eliot, *The Mill on the Floss*, Cabinet edition (Edinburgh and London: William Blackwood, 1878–80), Bk. I, ch. 1.

42. Although Eliot had been interested in phrenology, she undoubtedly now shared the scepticism towards some of its claims voiced by Lewes in *The Biographical History of Philosophy*. Lewes acknowledged the contribution of phrenology's founder, F. J. Gall, in proving that the brain was the organ of the mind, and that it was divided into separate organs. He dismissed as mere speculation, however, any attempt to read character from the surface of the skull, and to link brain capacity to size. See note 7 to ch. 1.

43. See note 8 to ch. 1. One can only surmise Eliot's reasons for its deletion, but it possibly came too close to her own voice, and to the representation of Tom Tulliver, thus breaking the illusion of Latimer's narration.

44. Eliot, *The Mill on the Floss*, Bk. IV, ch. 1.

45. Ibid., Bk. VI, ch. 14.

46. Entry of 2 January 1858, *Journals*, p. 73. Eliot notes she read to Lewes 'the delicious scenes at Tetterby's with the "Moloch of a baby" in the "Haunted Man"'.

47. See Sally Shuttleworth, '"The malady of thought": embodied memory in Victorian psychology and the novel', *Australasian Victorian Studies Journal* 2 (1996), pp. 1–12, reprinted M. Campbell, J. Labbe and S. Shuttleworth

(eds.), *Memory and Memorials, 1789–1914* (Routledge: London, 2000), pp. 46–59.

48. See Beryl Gray, 'Afterword', *The Lifted Veil* (London: Virago, 1985), pp. 83–4. Combe and Eliot had an extensive correspondence in 1852–4, and Eliot paid a two-week visit to Combe in October 1852, but the friendship was broken off when Combe reacted with horror to Eliot's liaison with Lewes. On 8 April 1852 Eliot had responded in a conciliatory way to Combe's accusation that the *Westmister Review*, which she was then editing, did not carry articles on mesmerism and phrenology. In fact it had carried a highly critical article on mesmerism in 1851 entitled 'Electro-Biology'. On 22 April Eliot wrote to Combe thanking him for the facts he had sent regarding Dr Gregory's patient, and expressing interest in the phenomenon of clairvoyance (*Letters*, VIII, 40–41; 43–6).

49. This case was discussed in 'New Discoveries in Ghosts' by Henry Morley in Dickens's *Household Words* 4 (17 January 1852). Morley was keen to offer a scientific explanation, suggesting that it was 'nothing supernatural, but a natural gift, imperceptible to us in its familar, moderate, and healthy exercise, brought first under our notice when some deranged adjustment of the mind has suffered it to grow into excess – to be, if we may call it so, a mental tumour' (pp. 404–5). See Louise Henson, 'Charles Dickens, Elizabeth Gaskell and Victorian Science', Ph.D. (University of Sheffield, 2000), p. 169.

50. Edgar Allan Poe, 'The Facts in the Case of M. Valdemar', *Tales of Adventure, Mystery and Imagination* (London: Ward, Lock and Co., 1891), p. 358. Poe's tale created a sensation in England, and elicited an eager response from Elizabeth Barrett (Michael Allen, *Poe and the British Magazine Tradition* (New York: Oxford University Press, 1969), p. 150).

51. Edward Bulwer-Lytton, 'The Haunted and the Haunters; or, the House and the Brain', *Blackwood's Edinburgh Magazine* 86 (August 1859), p. 263.

52. A. L. Wigan, *The Duality of Mind* (London: Longman, Brown, Green and Longman, 1844), p. 84. This work was in Lewes and Eliot's library (now held at Dr Williams's Library). Although Wigan's arguments were never fully accepted, his ideas none the less continued to be cited with respect throughout the century. (Wigan had dedicated his book to Henry Holland.)

53. Henry Holland, *Chapters on Mental Physiology* (London: Longman, Brown, Green and Longman, 1852), p. 198. Holland's text figures extensively in Lewes's *The Physiology of Common Life*. See Shuttleworth, '"The malady of thought"', pp. 51–7.

54. See Lewes, *The Physiology of Common Life*, II, 366–8.

55. See also Latimer's later comment that 'all the cramped, hemmed-in belief and disbelief, trust and distrust, of my nature, welled out in this one narrow channel' (ch. 2).

56. Lewes illustrates the ways in which attention controls perception through

the image of a mill wheel. He also argues that it is possible to have sensations without being conscious of them (*The Physiology of Common Life*, II, 59–60).

57. George Eliot, *Daniel Deronda*, Cabinet edition (Edinburgh and London: William Blackwood, 1878–80), Bk. I, ch. 1.

58. Mordecai's powers of prevision are linked to those of a scientific experimenter who foreshadows results 'in the fervour of concentrated prevision' (Bk. II, ch. 11). For a discussion of this point see Sally Shuttleworth, *George Eliot and Nineteenth-Century Science: The Make-believe of a Beginning* (Cambridge: Cambridge University Press, 1984), pp. 180–81. A more negative form of prevision is displayed by Gwendolen who seems to take over attributes of Latimer as well as Bertha. Like Latimer she is paralysed by her prevision which is fulfilled by her husband's death.

59. Eliot, *Daniel Deronda*, Bk. I, ch. 11.

60. Eliot casts Bertha's negative attributes on to Gwendolen's masculine partner, Grandcourt, who displays in greater depth the cruelty and lust for mastery exhibited by Bertha. He also shows the same inability to comprehend his partner's feelings and motivations due to his own limited emotional range and imagination. See *Daniel Deronda*, Bk. III, ch. 56.

61. Lewes worked with the chemist Justus von Liebig and the physiologist Karl von Siebold. See Rosemary Ashton, *G. H. Lewes: A Life* (Oxford: Clarendon Press, 1991), pp. 189–90, and William Baker (ed.), *The Letters of George Henry Lewes*, 2 vols., English Literary Studies Monograph Series no. 64 (Victoria, Canada: University of Victoria, 1995), I, 279.

62. G. H. Lewes, *Sea-side Studies*, 2nd edn (Edinburgh and London, 1860), p. 392.

63. G. H. Lewes, 'Circulation of the blood: its course and history', *Blackwood's Edinburgh Magazine* 84 (August 1858), p. 162.

64. Ibid., p. 160.

65. Ibid.

66. G. H. Lewes, 'Voluntary and involuntary actions', *Blackwood's Edinburgh Magazine* 86 (September 1859), p. 306. This material also formed part of *The Physiology of Common Life*, II, ch. 9. The precise chronology of the composition of the latter is unclear. On 17 June 1859 (*Lewes Ms Journal*), however, Lewes records in his diary that he began work on 'Sleep and Dreams' which forms II, ch. 11. This would suggest that he probably wrote the veil passage about the same time that Eliot was writing her story.

67. Kate Flint, 'Blood, bodies and *The Lifted Veil*', *Nineteenth-Century Literature* 51 (Spring 1997), pp. 455–73.

68. G. H. Lewes, 'Blood', *Blackwood's Edinburgh Magazine* 83 (June 1858), p. 699. Lewes's interest in Brown-Séquard's work also covered other areas germane to 'The Lifted Veil'. His copy of Brown-Séquard's 'Course of Lectures on the Physiology and Pathology of the Central Nervous System', delivered at the

Royal College of Surgeons, May 1858, and published in the *Lancet* from 3 July 1858 (now held at Dr Williams's Library), is extensively annotated. The 31 July issue is heavily marked with reference to the vivisection of dogs, and Lewes notes: 'What is the sign of sensibility? Because after he *completes* section of the chord all signs of sensibility are manifest.' Lewes's letter on 'Regeneration of the Spinal Chord' in frogs followed directly the conclusion of the Brown-Séquard lectures in the *Lancet* (25 December 1858). See also note 14 to ch. 2.

69. G. H. Lewes, 'Food and drink – Part II', *Blackwood's Edinburgh Magazine* 83 (April 1858), p. 404.

70. See Ludmilla Jordanova, *Sexual Visions: Images of Gender in Science and Medicine between the Eighteenth and Twentieth Centuries* (London: Harvester Wheatsheaf, 1989).

71. Lewes placed great emphasis on the fact that circulation of the blood was dependent on respiration. See 'Circulation of the blood', p. 163.

72. Eliot uses the general term 'artificial respiration'. It is unclear whether she intended mouth-to-mouth respiration, which had been popular in the eighteenth century until its safety was questioned by Joseph Priestley, or the less intimate action of exerting pressure on the chest, introduced by Marshall Hall in 1855.

73. Gilbert and Gubar read it as evidence of Eliot's self-division and self-hatred, the text as a whole showing what is also implied in Eliot's major fiction: 'that female power has been subverted into self-hatred which has deformed female creativity' (*The Madwoman in the Attic*, p. 477). Mary Jacobus, in *Reading Woman: Essays in Feminist Criticism* (London: Methuen, 1986), pp. 254–74, offers a psycho-analytic reading which links it to male hysterical fantasies about the castrating woman, and the tale as a whole to the condition of the woman writer under patriarchy.

74. Eliot was to learn, to her amusement, that the transfusion scene formed the basis of a painting by H. E. Blanchon, exhibited at the Paris Salon in May 1879. She wrote to her stepson Charles Lee Lewes on 10 June 1879: 'Fancy! Mrs Pattison has sent me word of a picture by a Fr[ench] artist in the Salon of this year, taken from the "Lifted Veil" – the moment when the resuscitated woman reveals her mistress's crime. Perhaps that hits the dominant French taste more than anything else of mine!' (*Letters*, VI, 163).

75. *Letters*, IV, 320; John Blackwood to George Eliot, 21 December 1866.

76. *Letters*, V, 380; to John Blackwood, 28 February 1873. The motto was adopted when 'The Lifted Veil' was reprinted as part of the Cabinet edition of Eliot's works, in 1878–80.

77. Its appeal for greater manhood, although clearly intended in a non-gender specific sense, none the less also compounds the gendered complexities of Eliot's position.

78. Eliot, *Daniel Deronda*, Bk. VI, ch. 41. See also note 58.

79. Entry for 27 September 1860; *Journals*, p. 86 (see A Note on the History of the Texts). In 1864, shortly before publication, she describes the story as 'only a trifle which I wrote 3 or 4 years ago, and have just given to Mr Smith because he wanted something for his forthcoming number of the Cornhill' (*Letters*, IV, 157; to Sara Hennell, 25 June 1864).

80. There is a large gap in her diary after the mention of the story, and she then notes on 28 November: 'Since I last wrote in this journal I have suffered much from physical weakness accompanied with mental depression' which 'has made me despair of ever working well again' (*Journals*, p. 87).

81. Lewes notes in his diary for 22 March 1859: 'In the evening Polly began Swift's Tale of a Tub, and read the beginning of her new story' (*Lewes Ms Journal*). In Section IX of 'A Tale of a Tub', 'A Digression concerning the Original, the Use, and Improvement of Madness in a Commonwealth', Swift notes:

Yesterday I ordered the carcass of a beau to be stripped in my presence, when we were all amazed to find so many unsuspected faults under one suit of clothes. Then I laid open his brain, his heart, and his spleen; but I plainly perceived at every operation, that the farther we proceeded, we found the defects increase upon us in number and bulk. (*Jonathan Swift: Gulliver's Travels and other Writings*, ed. Louis A. Landa (Oxford: Oxford University Press, 1976), p. 333)

82. Swift, *Gulliver's Travels*, p. 333.

83. Idiot was a term to be found in medical textbooks and common parlance at this time. Medical explanations of the various conditions grouped under this general label were only just beginning to be explored.

84. *Letters*, III, 294; 18 May 1860.

85. *Essays*, pp. 309, 323, 317. The link between sugar and poor literature recurs throughout Eliot's work: Philip in *The Mill on the Floss* dismisses Haydn's 'Creation', rather perversely one might think, as a 'sugared complacency' (Bk. VI, ch. 1), while Lydgate in *Middlemarch* describes Rosamond's fashionable *Keepsake* album as a 'sugared invention' (Bk. IV, ch. 27).

86. *Essays*, pp. 323, 322.

87. Eliot refers in a later part of the tale to a letter in the *Spectator* of 15 July 1712 (see ch. 2 and note 25). This would support the suggestion that her source for the 'Inkle and Yarico' story was the *Spectator*, and not one of the many later renditions (see note 7 to ch. 1).

88. Henry Morley (ed.), *The Spectator* (London: George Routledge and Sons, n.d.), p. 20. See also note 7 to ch. 1.

89. *Essays*, p. 322. Although Currer Bell had long been unmasked, Eliot respectfully employs the masculine name she had chosen for herself.

90. When the identity of Eliot was still wrapped in secrecy, rumours circulated that Joseph Liggins of Nuneaton was the author of her works, rumours he refused to deny. She was greatly upset by this deceit, and composed a letter to *The Times* (which Blackwood persuaded her not to publish), denouncing Liggins as an '*impostor*' and a '*swindler*' (*Letters*, III, 93; 25 June 1859). Rosemarie Bodenheimer has suggested that Eliot was creating in Faux a version of how her persecutors saw her own story: she stole family secrets, and then, as with the guineas, exhumed them 'in the form of consumable art' (*The Real Life of Mary Ann Evans: George Eliot, Her Letters and Fiction* (Ithaca, NY: Cornell University Press, 1994), p. 3). This line of argument is developed further by Susan de Sola Rodstein, 'Sweetness and dark: George Eliot's "Brother Jacob"', *Modern Language Quarterly* 52 (1991), pp. 309–17.

91. Morley, *The Spectator*, p. 21.

92. For a further exploration of the links of the tale to contemporary political economy, see Peter Allan Dale, 'George Eliot's "Brother Jacob": fables and the physiology of common life', *Philological Quarterly* 64 (1985), pp. 22–4.

93. It is unclear precisely when the tale is set. The reference to Mrs Steene's literary taste, however, cites poems published 1814–17. Since David Faux does not have the advantages of the Mechanics' Institutes, which were started around the country from the mid-1820s onwards, it would seem probable that the tale is set in the late 1820s or early 1830s, also when *The Mill on the Floss* is set. (Slavery was partially abolished in 1834, and transformed into an 'apprenticeship' system; it was fully abolished in 1838.)

94. Charles Dickens and Harriet Martineau published enthusiastic articles on these developments (respectively, 'Idiots', *Household Words* 7 (14 June 1853), pp. 313–17; and 'Idiots Again', *Household Words* 9 (15 April 1854), pp. 197–200). For further discussion of the role of idiots in nineteenth-century literature, see Sally Shuttleworth, '"So childish and so dreadfully un-childlike": cultural constructions of idiocy in the mid-nineteenth century', in Julie Scanlon and Amy Waste (eds.), *Crossing Boundaries* (Sheffield: Sheffield Academic Press, 2001).

95. Grandcourt's servant finds his movements as baffling as those of an insect (*Daniel Deronda*, Bk. IV, ch. 25). As the epigraph to that chapter suggests, 'How trace the why and wherefore in a mind reduced to the barenness of a fastidious egoism, in which all direct desires are dulled, and have dwindled from motives into a vacillating expectation of motives' (ibid.).

96. G. H. Lewes, 'Uncivilised Man', *Blackwood's Edinburgh Magazine* 89 (January 1861), p. 39.

97. This theory was most distinctly formulated in Spencer's essay 'Progress: its law and its cause', in *Essays: Scientific, Political and Speculative*, First Series (London: Longman, Brown, Green, Longman, and Roberts, 1858).

98. Herbert Spencer, 'The social organism', in *Essays: Scientific, Political and Speculative*, 3 vols. (London: Williams and Norgate, 1891), I, p. 294.

99. In *Sea-side Studies* (p. 60), Lewes had used the notion of the division of labour to explain the development of organic life.

100. H. T. Buckle, *History of Civilization in England*, 2 vols. (London: J. W. Parker & Son, 1857–61). Eliot expressed vehement opposition to this work in her letters, since Buckle held that 'there is no such thing as *race* or *hereditary transmission* of qualities' and argued that 'the progress of mankind is dependent entirely on the progress of knowledge, and that there has been no intrinsically-moral advance' (*Letters*, II, 415; to Charles Bray, 23 December 1857). Lewes noted in his diary that he reread this work on 17 February 1858 and made very similar observations, which were to form the crux of his argument in 'Mr Buckle's scientific errors', *Blackwood's Edinburgh Magazine* 90 (1861), 582–96.

101. Eliot, *The Mill on the Floss*, Bk, IV, ch. 1.

102. The famous anti-slavery slogan was used in a medallion struck by Wedgwood (1787), and also lay behind Cruikshank's 'Peterloo Medal' engraving where the image of the abject kneeling slave was transposed into that of a weaver. For details of some of the *Punch* cartoons, see Richard D. Altick, *Punch: The Lively Youth of a British Institution 1841–1851* (Columbus: Ohio State University Press, 1997), pp. 266–9.

103. *Adam Bede*, Cabinet edition (Edinburgh and London: William Blackwood, 1878–80), Bk. I, ch. 12.

104. Ibid., Bk. I, ch. 16.

105. *Letters*, III, 67; John Blackwood to George Eliot, 18 May 1859. One of the story's first critics, Henry James, actually preferred 'Brother Jacob' with its 'humorous cast' to the 'wofully sombre' 'Lifted Veil'. He praised the fine writing in both stories, observing that 'if they were interesting for nothing else, these two tales would be interesting as the *jeux d'esprit* of a mind that is not often – perhaps not often enough – found at play' (*Nation* 26 (25 April 1878), p. 277; reprinted in Gordon S. Haight (ed.), *A Century of George Eliot Criticism* (London: Methuen, 1965), pp. 130–31).

FURTHER READING

Primary Material

A. S. Byatt and Nicholas Warren (eds.), *George Eliot: Selected Essays, Poems and Other Writings* (Harmondsworth: Penguin, 1990).
Gordon S. Haight (ed.), *The George Eliot Letters*, 9 vols. (New Haven: Yale University Press, 1954–78).
Margaret Harris and Judith Johnston (eds.), *The Journals of George Eliot* (Cambridge: Cambridge University Press, 1998).
Thomas Pinney (ed.), *Essays of George Eliot* (New York: Columbia University Press, 1963).

Contemporary Review

Henry James, '"The Lifted Veil" and "Brother Jacob"', *Nation* 26 (25 April 1878), p. 277; reprinted in Gordon S. Haight (ed.), *A Century of George Eliot Criticism* (London: Methuen, 1965), p. 131.

Critical and Biographical Studies of Eliot's Stories

Rosemary Ashton, *George Eliot: A Life* (London: Hamish Hamilton, 1996).
Gillian Beer, 'Myth and the single consciousness: *Middlemarch* and *The Lifted Veil*', in Ian Adam (ed.), *This Particular Web: Essays on Middlemarch* (Toronto: Toronto University Press, 1975), pp. 91–115.
——, *George Eliot* (Brighton: Harvester, 1986).
Rosemarie Bodenheimer, *The Real Life of Mary Ann Evans: George Eliot, Her Letters and Fiction* (Ithaca, NY: Cornell University Press, 1994).
Kirstin Brady, *George Eliot* (London: Macmillan, 1992).

Malcolm Bull, 'Mastery and slavery in *The Lifted Veil*', *Essays in Criticism* 48 (1998), pp. 244–61.

David Carroll, *George Eliot and the Conflict of Interpretations* (Cambridge: Cambridge University Press, 1992).

Peter Allan Dale, 'George Eliot's "Brother Jacob": fables and the physiology of common life', *Philological Quarterly* 64 (1985), pp. 17–35.

Susan de Sola Rodstein, 'Sweetness and dark: George Eliot's "Brother Jacob"', *Modern Language Quarterly* 52 (1991), pp. 295–317.

Terry Eagleton, 'Power and knowledge in *The Lifted Veil*', *Literature and History* 9 (1983), pp. 52–61.

Kate Flint, 'Blood, bodies and *The Lifted Veil*', *Nineteenth-Century Literature* 51 (1997), pp. 455–73.

Richard Freedman, *Eliot, James and the Fictional Self: A Study in Character and Narrative* (London: Macmillan, 1986).

Sandra M. Gilbert and Susan Gubar, *The Madwoman in the Attic: The Woman Writer and the Nineteenth-Century Literary Imagination* (New Haven: Yale University Press, 1979).

Beryl M. Gray, 'Pseudoscience and George Eliot's "The Lifted Veil"', *Nineteenth-Century Fiction* 36 (1982), pp. 407–23.

——, Afterword to *The Lifted Veil* (London: Virago, 1985).

——, Afterword to *Brother Jacob* (London: Virago, 1989).

Gordon S. Haight, *George Eliot: A Biography* (Oxford: Oxford University Press, 1968).

Mary Jacobus, *Reading Woman: Essays in Feminist Criticism* (London: Methuen, 1986).

Frederick Karl, *George Eliot: A Biography* (London: Harper Collins, 1995).

U. C. Knoepflmacher, *George Eliot's Early Novels: The Limits of Realism* (Berkeley: University of California Press, 1968).

William Myers, *The Teaching of George Eliot* (Leicester: Leicester University Press, 1984).

Ruby Redinger, *George Eliot: The Emergent Self* (London: Bodley Head, 1975).

Sally Shuttleworth, *George Eliot and Nineteenth-Century Science: The Make-believe of a Beginning* (Cambridge: Cambridge University Press, 1984).

Charles Swann, 'Déja vu: déja lu: "The Lifted Veil" as an experiment in art', *Literature and History* 5 (1979), pp. 40–57.

Jenny Uglow, *George Eliot* (London: Virago, 1987).

Carroll Viera, '"The Lifted Veil" and George Eliot's early aesthetic', *Studies in English Literature* 24 (1984), pp. 749–67.

Alexander Welsh, *George Eliot and Blackmail* (Cambridge: Harvard University Press, 1985).

Judith Wilt, *Ghosts of the Gothic: Austen, Eliot, and Lawrence* (Princeton: Princeton University Press, 1980).

Hugh Witemeyer, 'George Eliot and Jean-Jacques Rousseau', *Comparative Literature Studies* 16 (1979), pp. 121–30.

Jane Wood, 'Scientific rationality and fanciful fiction: gendered discourse in *The Lifted Veil*', *Women's Writing* 3 (1996), pp. 161–76.

A NOTE ON THE HISTORY
OF THE TEXTS

'The Lifted Veil' was written during the first months of 1859, and was completed on 26 April. It was first published anonymously in *Blackwood's Edinburgh Magazine* 86 (July 1859), see Introduction and note 3. Eliot received £37.10 for it.

When Blackwood was preparing a cheap edition of Eliot's works in 1866, Eliot asked him to include both 'The Lifted Veil' and 'Brother Jacob', but he declined: 'my advice is against including them in the recognised series of your works' (*Letters*, IV, 320). In 1873, when he asked her if he could include 'The Lifted Veil' in a series of 'Tales from *Blackwood's*', she in turn declined. She did enclose a motto which was subsequently included as the epigraph when the tale was published in the Cabinet edition in 1878. Even at this stage, negotiations with Blackwood were not straightforward. Eliot had written to Blackwood on 30 January 1877, stating that she wished to add 'The Lifted Veil' and 'Brother Jacob' to the volume containing *Silas Marner*.[1] Blackwood tactfully replied that *Silas Marner* was 'such a perfect thing' that he wished to keep it in a volume on its own. Writing to her partner, G. H. Lewes, a month later he was more forthright: 'The Lifted Veil and Brother Jacob are wonderful Tales but both so desperately painful that I have a scruple in coupling them with Silas. Mrs Lewes and you however are by far the best judges of this'. Eliot's judgment prevailed, and the three were published together.[2]

Eliot revised the text of 'The Lifted Veil' slightly for the Cabinet edition, which forms the basis of this edition; she deleted one short passage, rewrote another, and generally made minor changes to punctuation, tense usage and word choice. Significant alterations are indicated in the Notes to this edition.

'Brother Jacob' was written after Eliot's return from a trip to Italy in the summer of 1860. She noted in her diary for 27 September: 'Since our return from Italy I have written a slight Tale – "Mr. David Faux, confectioner" – which G. thinks worth publishing.'[3] It was offered under the title of 'The Idiot Brother', and at a steep price of £250, to Sampson Low who had been pressing for some work from her, but was declined. Eliot does not seem to have had further thoughts about publishing the tale until 1862 when she noted in her diary for 7 February: 'The other day Mr. G. Smith called and offered me 250 guineas for my story of the Idiot Brother, which George mentioned as lying by me. I am not quite certain whether I shall accept.' The tale was too short for the three-part publication Smith had in mind for his new literary periodical, *Cornhill Magazine*. It was finally published in its entirety in the July 1864 edition of the *Cornhill* (Volume 10), complete with an illustrated frontispiece and initial letter drawing by Charles Swain. Eliot gave it as a gift to Smith who had suffered losses following his magnificent payment of £7000 to Eliot for the serial publication of *Romola* in the *Cornhill*.

'Brother Jacob' was not republished until its inclusion in the Cabinet edition of 1878. Eliot revised the text even more lightly than 'The Lifted Veil'. Punctuation was altered, some colloquial expressions were rendered more formal and word choice was revised occasionally. The Cabinet edition has again been used as the basis of this text, with significant alterations indicated in the Notes.

Notes

1. *Letters*, VI, 336.
2. *Letters*, VI, 340, 349.
3. *Journals*, p. 86.
4. *Journals*, p. 109.

The Lifted Veil

Give me no light, great Heaven, but such as turns
To energy of human fellowship ;
No powers beyond the growing heritage
That makes completer manhood.[1]

The time of my end approaches. I have lately been subject to attacks of *angina pectoris;*[1] and in the ordinary course of things, my physician tells me, I may fairly hope that my life will not be protracted many months. Unless, then, I am cursed with an exceptional physical constitution, as I am cursed with an exceptional mental character, I shall not much longer groan under the wearisome burthen of this earthly existence. If it were to be otherwise – if I were to live on to the age most men desire and provide for – I should for once have known whether the miseries of delusive expectation can outweigh the miseries of true prevision. For I foresee when I shall die, and everything that will happen in my last moments.

Just a month from this day, on the 20th of September 1850, I shall be sitting in this chair, in this study, at ten o'clock at night, longing to die, weary of incessant insight and foresight, without delusions and without hope. Just as I am watching a tongue of blue flame rising in the fire, and my lamp is burning low, the horrible contraction will begin at my chest. I shall only have time to reach the bell, and pull it violently, before the sense of suffocation will come. No one will answer my bell. I know why. My two servants are lovers, and will have quarrelled. My housekeeper will have rushed out of the house in a fury, two hours before, hoping that Perry will believe she has gone to drown herself. Perry is alarmed at last, and is gone out after her. The little scullery-maid is asleep on a bench: she never answers the bell; it does not wake her. The sense of suffocation increases: my lamp goes out with a horrible stench: I make a great effort, and snatch at the bell again. I long for life, and there is no help. I thirsted for the unknown: the thirst is gone. O God, let me stay with the known, and be weary of it: I am content. Agony of pain and suffocation – and all the while the earth, the fields, the pebbly brook at the bottom of the rookery, the fresh scent after the rain, the light of the morning through my chamber-window, the warmth of the hearth after the frosty air – will darkness close over them for ever?

Darkness – darkness – no pain – nothing but darkness: but I am passing on and on through the darkness: my thought stays in the darkness, but always with a sense of moving onward. . . .

Before that time comes, I wish to use my last hours of ease and strength in telling the strange story of my experience. I have never fully unbosomed myself to any human being; I have never been encouraged to trust much in the sympathy of my fellow-men. But we have all a chance of meeting with some pity, some tenderness, some charity, when we are dead: it is the living only who cannot be forgiven – the living only from whom men's indulgence and reverence are held off, like the rain by the hard east wind. While the heart beats, bruise it – it is your only opportunity; while the eye can still turn towards you with moist timid entreaty, freeze it with an icy unanswering gaze; while the ear, that delicate messenger to the inmost sanctuary of the soul, can still take in the tones of kindness, put it off with hard civility, or sneering compliment, or envious affectation of indifference; while the creative brain can still throb with the sense of injustice, with the yearning for brotherly recognition – make haste – oppress it with your ill-considered judgments, your trivial comparisons, your careless misrepresentations. The heart will by-and-by be still – *ubi sæva indignatio ulterius cor lacerare nequit;*[*2] the eye will cease to entreat; the ear will be deaf; the brain will have ceased from all wants as well as from all work. Then your charitable speeches may find vent; then you may remember and pity the toil and the struggle and the failure; then you may give due honour to the work achieved; then you may find extenuation for errors, and may consent to bury them.

That is a trivial schoolboy text; why do I dwell on it? It has little reference to me, for I shall leave no works behind me for men to honour. I have no near relatives who will make up, by weeping over my grave, for the wounds they inflicted on me when I was among them. It is only the story of my life that will perhaps win a little more sympathy from strangers when I am dead, than I ever believed it would obtain from my friends while I was living.

My childhood perhaps seems happier to me than it really was, by contrast with all the after-years. For then the curtain of the future was as impenetrable to me as to other children: I had all their delight in

* Inscription on Swift's tombstone.

the present hour, their sweet indefinite hopes for the morrow; and I had a tender mother: even now, after the dreary lapse of long years, a slight trace of sensation accompanies the remembrance of her caress as she held me on her knee – her arms round my little body, her cheek pressed on mine. I had a complaint of the eyes that made me blind for a little while, and she kept me on her knee from morning till night. That unequalled love soon vanished out of my life, and even to my childish consciousness it was as if that life had become more chill. I rode my little white pony with the groom by my side as before, but there were no loving eyes looking at me as I mounted, no glad arms opened to me when I came back. Perhaps I missed my mother's love[3] more than most children of seven or eight would have done, to whom the other pleasures of life remained as before; for I was certainly a very sensitive child. I remember still the mingled trepidation and delicious excitement with which I was affected by the tramping of the horses on the pavement in the echoing stables, by the loud resonance of the grooms' voices, by the booming bark of the dogs as my father's carriage thundered under the archway of the courtyard, by the din of the gong as it gave notice of luncheon and dinner. The measured tramp of soldiery which I sometimes heard – for my father's house lay near a county town where there were large barracks – made me sob and tremble; and yet when they were gone past, I longed for them to come back again.

I fancy my father thought me an odd child, and had little fondness for me; though he was very careful in fulfilling what he regarded as a parent's duties. But he was already past the middle of life, and I was not his only son. My mother had been his second wife, and he was five-and-forty when he married her. He was a firm, unbending, intensely orderly man, in root and stem a banker, but with a flourish-ing graft of the active landholder, aspiring to county influence: one of those people who are always like themselves from day to day, who are uninfluenced by the weather, and neither know melancholy nor high spirits. I held him in great awe, and appeared more timid and sensitive in his presence than at other times; a circumstance which, perhaps, helped to confirm him in the intention to educate me on a different plan from the prescriptive one with which he had complied in the case of my elder brother, already a tall youth at Eton. My brother was to be his representative and successor; he must go to Eton and Oxford, for the sake of making connections, of course: my father was not a man to underrate the bearing of Latin satirists or Greek dramatists on the attainment of an aristocratic position. But, intrinsically, he had slight esteem for 'those dead but sceptred spirits;'[4] having qualified himself for forming an independent opinion by reading Potter's 'Æschylus,' and dipping into Francis's 'Horace.'[5] To this negative view he added a positive one, derived, from a recent connection with mining specu-lations;[6] namely, that a scientific education was the really useful train-ing for a younger son. Moreover, it was clear that a shy, sensitive boy like me was not fit to encounter the rough experience of a public school. Mr Letherall[7] had said so very decidedly. Mr Letherall was a large man in spectacles, who one day took my small head between his large hands, and pressed it here and there in an exploratory, suspicious manner – then placed each of his great thumbs on my temples, and pushed me a little way from him, and stared at me with glittering spectacles. The contemplation appeared to displease him, for he frowned sternly, and said to my father, drawing his thumbs across my eyebrows –

'The deficiency is there, sir – there; and here,' he added, touching the upper sides of my head, 'here is the excess. That must be brought out, sir, and this must be laid to sleep.'

I was in a state of tremor, partly at the vague idea that I was the object of reprobation, partly in the agitation of my first hatred – hatred of this big, spectacled man, who pulled my head about as if he wanted to buy and cheapen it.

I am not aware how much Mr Letherall had to do with the system afterwards adopted towards me, but it was presently clear that private tutors, natural history, science, and the modern languages, were the appliances by which the defects of my organisation were to be rem-edied. I was very stupid about machines, so I was to be greatly occupied with them; I had no memory for classification, so it was particularly necessary that I should study systematic zoology and botany; I was hungry for human deeds and human emotions, so I was to be plentifully crammed with the mechanical powers, the elementary bodies, and the phenomena of electricity and magnetism. A better-constituted boy would certainly have profited under my intelligent tutors, with their scientific apparatus; and would, doubtless, have found the phenomena of electricity and magnetism as fascinating as I was, every Thursday, assured they were. As it was, I could have paired off, for ignorance of whatever was taught me, with the worst Latin scholar that was ever turned out of a classical academy.[8] I read Plutarch, and Shakspere, and Don Quixote[9] by the sly, and supplied myself in that way with wandering thoughts, while my tutor was assuring me that 'an improved man, as distinguished from an ignorant one, was a man who knew the reason why water ran down-hill.' I had no desire to be this improved man; I was glad of the running water; I could watch it and listen to it gurgling among the pebbles, and bathing the bright green water-plants, by the hour together. I did not want to know *why* it ran; I had perfect confidence that there were good reasons for what was so very beautiful.

There is no need to dwell on this part of my life. I have said enough to indicate that my nature was of the sensitive, unpractical order, and that it grew up in an uncongenial medium,[10] which could never foster it into happy, healthy development. When I was sixteen I was sent to Geneva[11] to complete my course of education; and the change was a very happy one to me, for the first sight of the Alps, with the setting sun on them, as we descended the Jura, seemed to me like an entrance into heaven; and the three years of my life there were spent in a perpetual sense of exaltation, as if from a draught of delicious wine, at the presence of Nature in all her awful loveliness. You will think, perhaps, that I must have been a poet, from this early sensibility to Nature. But my lot was not so happy as that. A poet pours forth his song and *believes* in the listening ear and answering soul, to which his song will be floated sooner or later. But the poet's sensibility without his voice – the poet's sensibility that finds no vent but in silent tears on the sunny bank, when the noonday light sparkles on the water, or in an inward shudder at the sound of harsh human tones, the sight of a cold human eye – this dumb passion brings with it a fatal solitude of soul in the society of one's fellow-men. My least solitary moments were those in which I pushed off in my boat, at evening, towards the centre of the lake; it seemed to me that the sky, and the glowing mountain-tops, and the wide blue water, surrounded me with a cherishing love such as no human face had shed on me since my mother's love had vanished out of my life. I used to do as Jean Jacques[12] did – lie down in my boat and let it glide where it would, while I looked up at the departing glow leaving one mountain-top after the other, as if the prophet's chariot of fire[13] were passing over them on its way to the home of light. Then, when the white summits were all sad and corpse-like, I had to push homeward, for I was under careful surveillance, and was allowed no late wanderings. This disposition of mine was not favourable to the formation of intimate friendships among the numerous youths of my own age who are always to be found studying at Geneva. Yet I made *one* such friendship; and, singularly enough, it was with a youth whose intellectual tendencies were the very reverse of my own. I shall call him Charles Meunier;[14] his real surname – an English one, for he was of English extraction – having since become celebrated. He was an orphan, who lived on a miserable pittance while he pursued the medical studies for which he had a special genius. Strange! that with my vague mind, susceptible and unobservant, hating inquiry and given up to contemplation, I should have been drawn towards a youth whose strongest passion was science. But the bond was not an intellectual one; it came from a source that can happily blend the stupid with the brilliant, the dreamy with the practical: it came from community of feeling. Charles was poor and ugly, derided by Genevese *gamins*,[15] and not acceptable in drawing-rooms. I saw that he was isolated, as I was, though from a different cause, and, stimulated by a sympathetic resentment, I made timid advances towards him. It is enough to say that there sprang up as much comradeship between us as our different habits would allow; and in Charles's rare holidays we went up the Salève together, or took the boat to Vevay,[16] while I listened dreamily to the monologues in which he unfolded his bold conceptions of future experiment and discovery. I mingled them confusedly in my thought with glimpses of blue water and delicate floating cloud, with the notes of birds and the distant glitter of the glacier. He knew quite well that my mind was half absent, yet he liked to talk to me in this way; for don't we talk of our hopes and our projects even to dogs and birds, when they love us? I have mentioned this one friendship because of its connection with a strange and terrible scene which I shall have to narrate in my subsequent life.

This happier life at Geneva was put an end to by a severe illness, which is partly a blank to me, partly a time of dimly-remembered suffering, with the presence of my father by my bed from time to time. Then came the languid monotony of convalescence, the days gradually breaking into variety and distinctness as my strength enabled me to take longer and longer drives. On one of these more vividly remembered days, my father said to me, as he sat beside my sofa –

'When you are quite well enough to travel, Latimer,[17] I shall take you home with me. The journey will amuse you and do you good, for I shall go through the Tyrol and Austria, and you will see many new places. Our neighbours, the Filmores, are come; Alfred will join us at Basle, and we shall all go together to Vienna, and back by Prague'. . . .

My father was called away before he had finished his sentence, and he left my mind resting on the word *Prague*, with a strange sense that a new and wondrous scene was breaking upon me: a city under the broad sunshine, that seemed to me as if it were the summer sunshine of a long-past century arrested in its course – unrefreshed for ages by the dews of night, or the rushing rain-cloud; scorching the dusty, weary, time-eaten grandeur of a people doomed to live on in the stale repetition of memories, like deposed and superannuated kings in their regal gold-inwoven tatters. The city looked so thirsty that the broad river seemed to me a sheet of metal; and the blackened statues, as I passed under their blank gaze, along the unending bridge,[18] with their ancient garments and their saintly crowns, seemed to me the real inhabitants and owners of this place, while the busy, trivial men and women, hurrying to and fro, were a swarm of ephemeral visitants infesting it for a day. It is such grim, stony beings as these, I thought, who are the fathers of ancient faded children, in those tanned time-fretted dwellings that crowd the steep before me; who pay their court in the worn and crumbling pomp of the palace which stretches its monotonous length on the height; who worship wearily in the stifling air of the churches, urged by no fear or hope, but compelled by their doom to be ever old and undying, to live on in the rigidity of habit, as they live on in perpetual mid-day, without the repose of night or the new birth of morning.

A stunning clang of metal suddenly thrilled through me, and I became conscious of the objects in my room again: one of the fire-irons had fallen as Pierre opened the door to bring me my draught.[19] My heart was palpitating violently, and I begged Pierre to leave my draught beside me; I would take it presently.

As soon as I was alone again, I began to ask myself whether I had been sleeping. Was this a dream – this wonderfully distinct vision – minute in its distinctness down to a patch of rainbow light on the pavement, transmitted through a coloured lamp in the shape of a star

– of a strange city, quite unfamiliar to my imagination? I had seen no picture of Prague: it lay in my mind as a mere name, with vaguely-remembered historical associations – ill-defined memories of imperial grandeur and religious wars.

Nothing of this sort had ever occurred in my dreaming experience before, for I had often been humiliated because my dreams were only saved from being utterly disjointed and commonplace by the frequent terrors of nightmare. [20] But I could not believe that I had been asleep, for I remembered distinctly the gradual breaking-in of the vision upon me, like the new images in a dissolving view,[21] or the growing distinctness of the landscape as the sun lifts up the veil of the morning mist. And while I was conscious of this incipient vision, I was also conscious that Pierre came to tell my father Mr Filmore was waiting for him, and that my father hurried out of the room. No, it was not a dream ; was it – the thought was full of tremulous exultation – was it the poet's nature in me, hitherto only a troubled yearning sensibility, now manifesting itself suddenly as spontaneous creation? Surely it was in this way that Homer saw the plain of Troy, that Dante saw the abodes of the departed, that Milton[22] saw the earthward flight of the Tempter. Was it that my illness had wrought some happy change in my organisation – given a firmer tension to my nerves – carried off some dull obstruction? I had often read of such effects – in works of fiction at least. Nay; in genuine biographies I had read of the subtilising or exalting influence of some diseases on the mental powers. Did not Novalis[23] feel his inspiration intensified under the progress of consumption?

When my mind had dwelt for some time on this blissful idea, it seemed to me that I might perhaps test it by an exertion of my will. The vision had begun when my father was speaking of our going to Prague. I did not for a moment believe it was really a representation of that city; I believed – I hoped it was a picture that my newly-liberated genius had painted in fiery haste, with the colours snatched from lazy memory. Suppose I were to fix my mind on some other place – Venice, for example, which was far more familiar to my imagination than Prague: perhaps the same sort of result would follow. I concentrated my thoughts on Venice; I stimulated my imagination with poetic memories, and strove to feel myself present in Venice, as I had felt myself present in Prague. But in vain. I was only colouring the Canaletto[24] engravings that hung in my old bedroom at home; the picture was a shifting one, my mind wandering uncertainly in search of more vivid images; I could see no accident of form or shadow without conscious labour after the necessary conditions. It was all prosaic effort, not rapt passivity, such as I had experienced half an hour before. I was discouraged; but I remembered that inspiration was fitful.

For several days I was in a state of excited expectation, watching for a recurrence of my new gift. I sent my thoughts ranging over my world of knowledge, in the hope that they would find some object which would send a reawakening vibration through my slumbering genius. But no; my world remained as dim as ever, and that flash of strange light refused to come again, though I watched for it with palpitating eagerness.

My father accompanied me every day in a drive, and a gradually lengthening walk as my powers of walking increased; and one evening he had agreed to come and fetch me at twelve the next day, that we might go together to select a musical box, and other purchases rigorously demanded of a rich Englishman visiting Geneva. He was one of the most punctual of men and bankers, and I was always nervously anxious to be quite ready for him at the appointed time. But, to my surprise, at a quarter past twelve he had not appeared. I felt all the impatience of a convalescent who has nothing particular to do, and who has just taken a tonic in the prospect of immediate exercise that would carry off the stimulus.

Unable to sit still and reserve my strength, I walked up and down the room, looking out on the current of the Rhone, just where it leaves the dark-blue lake; but thinking all the while of the possible causes that could detain my father.

Suddenly I was conscious that my father was in the room, but not alone: there were two persons with him. Strange! I had heard no footstep, I had not seen the door open; but I saw my father, and at his right hand our neighbour Mrs Filmore, whom I remembered very well, though I had not seen her for five years. She was a commonplace middle-aged woman, in silk and cashmere; but the lady on the left of my father was not more than twenty, a tall, slim, willowy figure, with luxuriant blond hair, arranged in cunning braids and folds that looked almost too massive for the slight figure and the small-featured, thin-lipped face they crowned. But the face had not a girlish expression: the features were sharp, the pale grey eyes at once acute, restless, and sarcastic. They were fixed on me in half-smiling curiosity, and I felt a painful sensation as if a sharp wind were cutting me. The pale-green dress, and the green leaves that seemed to form a border about her pale blond hair, made me think of a Water-Nixie,[25] – for my mind was full of German lyrics, and this pale, fatal-eyed woman, with the green weeds, looked like a birth from some cold sedgy stream, the daughter of an aged river.

'Well, Latimer, you thought me long,' my father said. . . .

But while the last word was in my ears, the whole group vanished, and there was nothing between me and the Chinese painted folding-screen that stood before the door. I was cold and trembling; I could only totter forward and throw myself on the sofa. This strange new power had manifested itself again. . . . But *was* it a power? Might it not rather be a disease – a sort of intermittent delirium, concentrating my energy of brain into moments of unhealthy activity, and leaving my saner hours all the more barren? I felt a dizzy sense of unreality in what my eye rested on; I grasped the bell convulsively, like one trying to free himself from nightmare, and rang it twice. Pierre came with a look of alarm in his face.

'Monsieur ne se trouve pas bien?'[26] he said, anxiously.

'I'm tired of waiting, Pierre,' I said, as distinctly and emphatically as I could, like a man determined to be sober in spite of wine; 'I'm afraid something has happened to my father – he's usually so punctual. Run to the Hôtel des Bergues[27] and see if he is there.'

Pierre left the room at once, with a soothing 'Bien, Monsieur;' and I felt the better for this scene of simple, waking prose. Seeking to calm myself still further, I went into my bedroom, adjoining the *salon*, and opened a case of eau-de-Cologne; took out a bottle; went through the process of taking out the cork very neatly, and then rubbed the reviving spirit over my hands and forehead, and under my nostrils, drawing a new delight from the scent because I had procured it by slow details of labour, and by no strange sudden madness. Already I had begun to taste something of the horror that belongs to the lot of a human being whose nature is not adjusted to simple human conditions.

Still enjoying the scent, I returned to the *salon*, but it was not unoccupied, as it had been before I left it. In front of the Chinese folding-screen there was my father, with Mrs Filmore on his right hand, and on his left—the slim blond-haired girl, with the keen face and the keen eyes fixed on me in half-smiling curiosity.

'Well, Latimer, you thought me long,' my father said. . . .

I heard no more, felt no more, till I became conscious that I was lying with my head low on the sofa, Pierre and my father by my side. As soon as I was thoroughly revived, my father left the room, and presently returned, saying –

'I've been to tell the ladies how you are, Latimer. They were waiting in the next room. We shall put off our shopping expedition to-day.'

Presently he said, 'That young lady is Bertha[28] Grant, Mrs Filmore's orphan niece. Filmore has adopted her, and she lives with them, so you will have her for a neighbour when we go home – perhaps for a near relation; for there is a tenderness between her and Alfred, I suspect, and I should be gratified by the match, since Filmore means to provide for her in every way as if she were his daughter. It had not occurred to me that you knew nothing about her living with the Filmores.'

He made no further allusion to the fact of my having fainted at the moment of seeing her, and I would not for the world have told him the reason: I shrank from the idea of disclosing to any one what might be regarded as a pitiable peculiarity, most of all from betraying it to my father, who would have suspected my sanity ever after.

I do not mean to dwell with particularity on the details of my experience. I have described these two cases at length, because they had definite, clearly traceable results in my after-lot.

Shortly after this last occurrence I – think the very next day – I began to be aware of a phase in my abnormal sensibility, to which, from the languid and slight nature of my intercourse with others since my illness, I had not been alive before. This was the obtrusion on my mind of the mental process going forward in first one person, and then another, with whom I happened to be in contact: the vagrant, frivolous ideas and emotions of some uninteresting acquaintance – Mrs Filmore, for example – would force themselves on my consciousness like an importunate, ill-played musical instrument, or the loud activity of an imprisoned insect. But this unpleasant sensibility was fitful, and left me moments of rest, when the souls of my companions were once more shut out from me, and I felt a relief such as silence brings to wearied nerves. I might have believed this importunate insight to be merely a diseased activity of the imagination, but that my prevision[29] of incalculable words and actions proved it to have a fixed relation to the mental process in other minds. But this superadded consciousness, wearying and annoying enough when it urged on me the trivial experience of indifferent people, became an intense pain and grief when it seemed to be opening to me the souls of those who were in a close relation to me – when the rational talk, the graceful attentions, the wittily-turned phrases, and the kindly deeds, which used to make the web of their characters, were seen as if thrust asunder by a microscopic vision, that showed all the intermediate frivolities, all the suppressed egoism, all the struggling chaos of puerilities, meanness, vague capricious memories, and indolent make-shift thoughts, from which human words and deeds emerge like leaflets covering a fermenting heap.

At Basle we were joined by my brother Alfred, now a handsome self-confident man of six-and-twenty – a thorough contrast to my fragile, nervous, ineffectual self. I believe I was held to have a sort of half-womanish, half-ghostly beauty; for the portrait-painters, who are thick as weeds at Geneva, had often asked me to sit to them, and I had been the model of a dying minstrel in a fancy picture.[30] But I thoroughly disliked my own *physique*, and nothing but the belief that it was a condition of poetic genius would have reconciled me to it. That brief hope was quite fled, and I saw in my face now nothing but the stamp of a morbid organisation, framed for passive suffering – too feeble for the sublime resistance of poetic production. Alfred, from whom I had been almost constantly separated, and who, in his present stage of character and appearance, came before me as a perfect stranger, was bent on being extremely friendly and brother-like to me. He had the superficial kindness of a good-humoured, self-satisfied nature, that fears no rivalry, and has encountered no contrarieties. I am not sure that my disposition was good enough for me to have been quite free from envy towards him, even if our desires had not clashed, and if I had been in the healthy human condition which admits of generous confidence and charitable construction. There must always have been an antipathy between our natures. As it was, he became in a few weeks an object of intense hatred to me; and when he entered the room, still more when he spoke, it was as if a sensation of grating metal had set my teeth on edge. My diseased consciousness was more intensely and continually occupied with his thoughts and emotions, than with those of any other person who came in my way. I was perpetually exasperated with the petty promptings of his conceit and his love of patronage, with his self-complacent belief in Bertha Grant's passion for him, with his half-pitying contempt for me – seen not in the ordinary indications of intonation and phrase and slight action, which an acute and suspicious mind is on the watch for, but in all their naked skinless complication.

For we were rivals, and our desires clashed, though he was not aware of it. I have said nothing yet of the effect Bertha Grant produced in me on a nearer acquaintance. That effect was chiefly determined by the fact that she made the only exception, among all the human beings about me, to my unhappy gift of insight. About Bertha I was always in a state of uncertainty: I could watch the expression of her face, and speculate on its meaning; I could ask for her opinion with the real interest of ignorance; I could listen for her words and watch for her smile with hope and fear: she had for me the fascination of an unravelled destiny. I say it was this fact that chiefly determined the strong effect she produced on me: for, in the abstract, no womanly character could seem to have less affinity[31] for that of a shrinking, romantic, passionate youth than Bertha's. She was keen, sarcastic, unimaginative, prematurely cynical, remaining critical and unmoved in the most impressive scenes, inclined to dissect all my favourite poems, and especially contemptuous towards the German lyrics[32] which were my pet literature at that time. To this moment I am unable to define my feeling towards her: it was not ordinary boyish admiration, for she was the very opposite, even to the colour of her hair, of the ideal woman who still remained to me the type of loveliness; and she was without that enthusiasm for the great and good, which, even at the moment of her strongest dominion over me, I should have declared to be the highest element of character. But there is no tyranny more complete than that which a self-centred negative nature exercises over a morbidly sensitive nature perpetually craving sympathy and support. The most independent people feel the effect of a man's silence in heightening their value for his opinion – feel an additional triumph in conquering the reverence of a critic habitually captious and satirical: no wonder, then, that an enthusiastic self-distrusting youth should watch and wait before the closed secret of a sarcastic woman's face, as if it were the shrine of the doubtfully benignant deity who ruled his destiny. For a young enthusiast is unable to imagine the total negation in another mind of the emotions which are stirring his own: they may be feeble, latent, inactive, he thinks, but they are there – they may be called forth; sometimes, in moments of happy hallucination, he believes they may be there in all the greater strength because he sees no outward sign of them. And this effect, as I have intimated, was heightened to its utmost intensity in me, because Bertha was the only being who remained for me in the mysterious seclusion of soul that renders such youthful delusion possible. Doubtless there was another sort of fascination at work – that subtle physical attraction which delights in cheating our psychological predictions, and in compelling the men who paint sylphs, to fall in love with some *bonne et brave femme*,[33] heavy-heeled and freckled.

Bertha's behaviour towards me was such as to encourage all my illusions, to heighten my boyish passion, and make me more and more dependent on her smiles. Looking back with my present wretched knowledge, I conclude that her vanity and love of power were intensely gratified by the belief that I had fainted on first seeing her purely from the strong impression her person had produced on me. The most prosaic woman likes to believe herself the object of a violent, a poetic passion; and without a grain of romance in her, Bertha had that spirit of intrigue which gave piquancy to the idea that the brother of the man she meant to marry was dying with love and jealousy for her sake. That she meant to marry my brother, was what at that time I did not believe; for though he was assiduous in his attentions to her, and I knew well enough that both he and my father had made up their minds to this result, there was not yet an understood engagement – there had been no explicit declaration; and Bertha habitually, while she flirted with my brother, and accepted his homage in a way that implied to him a thorough recognition of its intention, made me believe, by the subtlest looks and phrases – feminine[34] nothings which could never be quoted against her – that he was really the object of her secret ridicule; that she thought him, as I did, a coxcomb, whom she would have pleasure in disappointing. Me she openly petted in my brother's presence, as if I were too young and sickly ever to be thought of as a lover; and that was the view he took of me. But I believe she must inwardly have delighted in the tremors into which she threw me by the coaxing way in which she patted my curls, while she laughed at my quotations. Such caresses were always given in the presence of our friends; for when we were alone together, she affected a much greater distance towards me, and now and then took the opportunity, by words or slight actions, to stimulate my foolish timid hope that she really preferred me. And why should she not follow her inclination? I was not in so advantageous a position as my brother, but I had fortune, I was not a year younger than she was, and she was an heiress, who would soon be of age to decide for herself.

The fluctuations of hope and fear, confined to this one channel, made each day in her presence a delicious torment. There was one deliberate act of hers which especially helped to intoxicate me. When we were at Vienna her twentieth birthday occurred, and as she was very fond of ornaments, we all took the opportunity of the splendid jewellers' shops in that Teutonic Paris to purchase her a birthday present of jewellery. Mine, naturally, was the least expensive; it was an opal[35] ring – the opal was my favourite stone, because it seems to blush and turn pale as if it had a soul. I told Bertha so when I gave it her, and said that it was an emblem of the poetic nature, changing with the changing light of heaven and of woman's eyes. In the evening she appeared elegantly dressed, and wearing conspicuously all the birthday presents except mine. I looked eagerly at her fingers, but saw no opal. I had no opportunity of noticing this to her during the evening; but the next day, when I found her seated near the window alone, after breakfast, I said, 'You scorn to wear my poor opal. I should have remembered that you despised poetic natures, and should have given you coral, or turquoise, or some other opaque unresponsive stone.' 'Do I despise it?' she answered, taking hold of a delicate gold chain which she always wore round her neck and drawing out the end from her bosom with my ring hanging to it; 'it hurts me a little, I can tell you,' she said, with her usual dubious smile, 'to wear it in that secret place; and since your poetical nature is so stupid as to prefer a more public position, I shall not endure the pain any longer.'

She took off the ring from the chain and put it on her finger, smiling still, while the blood rushed to my cheeks, and I could not trust myself to say a word of entreaty that she would keep the ring where it was before.

I was completely fooled by this, and for two days shut myself up in my own room whenever Bertha was absent, that I might intoxicate myself afresh with the thought of this scene and all it implied.

I should mention that during these two months – which seemed a long life to me from the novelty and intensity of the pleasures and pains I underwent – my diseased participation in other people's consciousness continued to torment me; now it was my father, and now my brother, now Mrs Filmore or her husband, and now our German courier, whose stream of thought rushed upon me like a ringing in the ears not to be got rid of, though it allowed my own impulses and ideas to continue their uninterrupted course. It was like a preternaturally heightened sense of hearing,[36] making audible to one a roar of sound where others find perfect stillness. The weariness and disgust of this involuntary intrusion into other souls was counteracted only by my ignorance of Bertha, and my growing passion for her; a passion enormously stimulated, if not produced, by that ignorance. She was my oasis of mystery in the dreary desert of knowledge. I had never allowed my diseased condition to betray itself, or to drive me into any unusual speech or action, except once, when, in a moment of peculiar bitterness against my brother, I had forestalled some words which I knew he was going to utter – a clever observation, which he had prepared beforehand. He had occasionally a slightly-affected hesitation in his speech, and when he paused an instant after the second word, my impatience and jealousy impelled me to continue the speech for him, as if it were something we had both learned by rote. He coloured and looked astonished, as well as annoyed; and the words had no sooner escaped my lips than I felt a shock of alarm lest such an anticipation of words – very far from being words of course, easy to divine – should have betrayed me as an exceptional being, a sort of quiet energumen,[37] whom every one, Bertha above all, would shudder at and avoid. But I magnified, as usual, the impression any word or deed of mine could produce on others; for no one gave any sign of having noticed my interruption as more than a rudeness, to be forgiven me on the score of my feeble nervous condition.

While this superadded consciousness of the actual was almost constant with me, I had never had a recurrence of that distinct prevision which I have described in relation to my first interview with Bertha; and I was waiting with eager curiosity to know whether or not my vision of Prague would prove to have been an instance of the same kind. A few days after the incident of the opal ring, we were paying one of our frequent visits to the Lichtenberg Palace.[38] I could never look at many pictures in succession; for pictures, when they are at all powerful, affect me so strongly that one or two exhaust all my capability of contemplation. This morning I had been looking at Giorgione's picture of the cruel-eyed woman, said to be a likeness of Lucrezia Borgia.[39] I had stood long alone before it, fascinated by the terrible reality of that cunning, relentless face, till I felt a strange poisoned sensation, as if I had long been inhaling a fatal odour, and was just beginning to be conscious of its effects. Perhaps even then I should not have moved away, if the rest of the party had not returned to this room, and announced that they were going to the Belvedere Gallery[40] to settle a bet which had arisen between my brother and Mr Filmore about a portrait. I followed them dreamily, and was hardly alive to what occurred till they had all gone up to the gallery, leaving me below; for I refused to come within sight of another picture that day. I made my way to the Grand Terrace,[41] since it was agreed that we should saunter in the gardens when the dispute had been decided. I had been sitting here a short space, vaguely conscious of trim gardens, with a city and green hills in the distance, when, wishing to avoid the proximity of the sentinel, I rose and walked down the broad stone steps, intending to seat myself farther on in the gardens. Just as I reached the gravel-walk, I felt an arm slipped within mine, and a light hand gently pressing my wrist. In the same instant a strange intoxicating numbness passed over me, like the continuance or climax of the sensation I was still feeling from the gaze of Lucrezia Borgia. The gardens, the summer sky, the consciousness of Bertha's arm being within mine, all vanished, and I seemed to be suddenly in darkness, out of which there gradually broke a dim firelight, and I felt myself sitting in my father's leather chair in the library at home. I knew the fireplace – the dogs[42] for the wood-fire – the black marble chimney-piece with the white marble medallion of the dying Cleopatra[43] in the centre. Intense and hopeless misery was pressing on my soul; the light became stronger, for Bertha was entering with a candle in her hand – Bertha, my wife – with cruel eyes, with green jewels and green leaves on her white ball-dress; every hateful thought within her present to me. . . . 'Madman, idiot! why don't you kill yourself, then?' It was a moment of hell. I saw into her pitiless soul – saw its barren worldliness, its scorching hate – and felt it clothe me round like an air I was obliged to breathe. She came with her candle and stood over me with a bitter smile of contempt; I saw the great emerald brooch on her bosom, a studded serpent with diamond eyes. I shuddered – I despised this woman with the barren soul and mean thoughts; but I felt helpless before her, as if she clutched my bleeding heart, and would clutch it till the last drop of life-blood ebbed away. She was my wife, and we hated each other. Gradually the hearth, the dim library, the candle-light disappeared – seemed to melt away into a background of light, the green serpent with the diamond eyes remaining a dark image on the retina. Then I had a sense of my eyelids quivering, and the living daylight broke in upon me; I saw gardens, and heard voices; I was seated on the steps of the Belvedere Terrace, and my friends were round me.

The tumult of mind into which I was thrown by this hideous vision made me ill for several days, and prolonged our stay at Vienna. I shuddered with horror as the scene recurred to me; and it recurred constantly, with all its minutiæ, as if they had been burnt into my memory; and yet, such is the madness of the human heart under the influence of its immediate desires, I felt a wild hell-braving joy that Bertha was to be mine; for the fulfilment of my former prevision concerning her first appearance before me, left me little hope that this last hideous glimpse of the future was the mere diseased play of my own mind, and had no relation to external realities. One thing alone I looked towards as a possible means of casting doubt on my terrible conviction – the discovery that my vision of Prague had been false – and Prague was the next city on our route.

Meanwhile, I was no sooner in Bertha's society again, than I was as completely under her sway as before. What if I saw into the heart of Bertha, the matured woman – Bertha, my wife? Bertha, the *girl*,[44] was a fascinating secret to me still: I trembled under her touch; I felt the witchery of her presence; I yearned to be assured of her love. The fear of poison is feeble against the sense of thirst. Nay, I was just as jealous of my brother as before – just as much irritated by his small patronising ways; for my pride, my diseased sensibility, were there as they had always been, and winced as inevitably under every offence as my eye winced from an intruding mote. The future, even when brought within the compass of feeling by a vision that made me shudder, had still no more than the force of an idea, compared with the force of present emotion – of my love for Bertha, of my dislike and jealousy towards my brother.

It is an old story,[45] that men sell themselves to the tempter, and sign a bond with their blood, because it is only to take effect at a distant day; then rush on to snatch the cup their souls thirst after with an impulse not the less savage[46] because there is a dark shadow beside them for evermore. There is no short cut, no patent tram-road,[47] to wisdom : after all the centuries of invention, the soul's path lies through the thorny wilderness[48] which must be still trodden in solitude, with bleeding feet, with sobs for help, as it was trodden by them of old time.

My mind speculated eagerly on the means by which I should become my brother's successful rival, for I was still too timid, in my ignorance of Bertha's actual feeling, to venture on any step that would urge from her an avowal of it. I thought I should gain confidence even for this, if my vision of Prague proved to have been veracious; and yet, the horror of that certitude! Behind the slim girl Bertha, whose words and looks I watched for, whose touch was bliss, there stood continually that Bertha with the fuller form, the harder eyes, the more rigid mouth, – with the barren selfish soul laid bare; no longer a fascinating secret, but a measured fact, urging itself perpetually on my unwilling sight. Are you unable to give me your sympathy – you who read this? Are you unable to imagine this double consciousness[49] at work within me, flowing on like two parallel streams which never mingle their waters and blend into a common hue? Yet you must have known something of the presentiments that spring from an insight at war with passion; and my visions were only like presentiments intensified to horror. You have known the powerlessness of ideas before the might of impulse; and my visions, when once they had passed into memory, were mere ideas – pale shadows that beckoned in vain, while my hand was grasped by the living and the loved.

In after-days I thought with bitter regret that if I had foreseen something more or something different – if instead of that hideous vision which poisoned the passion it could not destroy, or if even along with it I could have had a foreshadowing of that moment when I looked on my brother's face for the last time, some softening influence would have been shed over my feeling towards him: pride and hatred would surely have been subdued into pity, and the record of those hidden sins would have been shortened. But this is one of the vain thoughts with which we men flatter ourselves. We try[50] to believe that the egoism within us would have easily been melted, and that it was only the narrowness of our knowledge which hemmed in our generosity, our awe, our human piety, and hindered them from submerging our hard indifference to the sensations and emotions of our fellow. Our tenderness and self-renunciation seem strong when our egoism[51] has had its day – when, after our mean striving for a triumph that is to be another's loss, the triumph comes suddenly, and we shudder at it, because it is held out by the chill hand of death.

Our arrival in Prague happened at night, and I was glad of this, for it seemed like a deferring of a terribly decisive moment, to be in the city for hours without seeing it. As we were not to remain long in Prague, but to go on speedily to Dresden, it was proposed that we should drive out the next morning and take a general view of the place, as well as visit some of its specially interesting spots, before the heat became oppressive – for we were in August, and the season was hot and dry. But it happened that the ladies were rather late at their morning toilet, and to my father's politely-repressed but perceptible annoyance, we were not in the carriage till the morning was far advanced. I thought with a sense of relief, as we entered the Jews' quarter, where we were to visit the old synagogue, that we should be kept in this flat, shut-up part of the city, until we should all be too tired and too warm to go farther, and so we should return without seeing more than the streets through which we had already passed. That would give me another day's suspense – suspense, the only form in which a fearful spirit knows the solace of hope. But, as I stood under the blackened, groined arches of that old synagogue, made dimly visible by the seven thin candles in the sacred lamp, while our Jewish cicerone[52] reached down the Book of the Law, and read to us in its ancient tongue, – I felt a shuddering impression that this strange building, with its shrunken lights, this surviving withered remnant of medieval Judaism, was of a piece with my vision. Those darkened dusty Christian saints, with their loftier arches and their larger candles, needed the consolatory scorn with which they might point to a more shrivelled death-in-life than their own.

As I expected, when we left the Jews' quarter the elders of our party wished to return to the hotel. But now, instead of rejoicing in this, as I had done beforehand, I felt a sudden overpowering impulse to go on at once to the bridge, and put an end to the suspense I had been wishing to protract. I declared, with unusual decision, that I would get out of the carriage and walk on alone; they might return without me. My father, thinking this merely a sample of my usual 'poetic nonsense,' objected that I should only do myself harm by walking in the heat; but when I persisted, he said angrily that I might follow my own absurd devices, but that Schmidt (our courier) must go with me. I assented to this, and set off with Schmidt towards the bridge. I had no sooner passed from under the archway of the grand old gate leading on to the bridge, than a trembling seized me, and I turned cold under the mid-day sun; yet I went on; I was in search of something – a small detail which I remembered with special intensity as part of my vision. There it was – the patch of rainbow light on the pavement transmitted through a lamp in the shape of a star.

CHAPTER 2

Before the autumn was at an end, and while the brown leaves still stood thick on the beeches in our park, my brother and Bertha were engaged to each other, and it was understood that their marriage was to take place early in the next spring. In spite of the certainty I had felt from that moment on the bridge at Prague, that Bertha would one day be my wife, my constitutional timidity and distrust had continued to benumb me, and the words in which I had sometimes premeditated a confession of my love, had died away unuttered. The same conflict had gone on within me as before – the longing for an assurance of love from Bertha's lips, the dread lest a word of contempt and denial should fall upon me like a corrosive acid. What was the conviction of a distant necessity to me? I trembled under a present glance, I hungered after a present joy, I was clogged and chilled by a present fear. And so the days passed on: I witnessed Bertha's engagement and heard her marriage discussed as if I were under a conscious nightmare – knowing it was a dream that would vanish, but feeling stifled under the grasp of hard-clutching fingers.

When I was not in Bertha's presence – and I was with her very often, for she continued to treat me with a playful patronage that wakened no jealousy in my brother – I spent my time chiefly in wandering, in strolling, or taking long rides while the daylight lasted, and then shutting myself up with my unread books; for books had lost the power of chaining my attention. My self-consciousness was heightened to that pitch of intensity in which our own emotions take the form of a drama[1] which urges itself imperatively on our contemplation, and we begin to weep, less under the sense of our suffering than at the thought of it. I felt a sort of pitying anguish over the pathos of my own lot: the lot of a being finely organised for pain, but with hardly any fibres that responded to pleasure – to whom the idea of future evil robbed the present of its joy, and for whom the idea of future good did not still the uneasiness of a present yearning or a present dread. I went dumbly through that stage of the poet's suffering, in which he feels the delicious pang of utterance, and makes an image of his sorrows.

I was left entirely without remonstrance concerning this dreamy wayward life: I knew my father's thought about me: 'That lad will never be good for anything in life: he may waste his years in an insignificant way on the income that falls to him: I shall not trouble myself about a career for him.'

One mild morning in the beginning of November, it happened that I was standing outside the portico patting lazy old Cæsar, a Newfoundland almost blind with age, the only dog that ever took any notice of me – for the very dogs shunned me, and fawned on the happier people about me – when the groom brought up my brother's horse which was to carry him to the hunt, and my brother himself appeared at the door, florid, broad-chested, and self-complacent, feeling what a good-natured fellow he was not to behave insolently to us all on the strength of his great advantages.

'Latimer, old boy,' he said to me in a tone of compassionate cordiality, 'what a pity it is you don't have a run with the hounds now and then! The finest thing in the world for low spirits!'

'Low spirits!' I thought bitterly, as he rode away; 'that is the sort of phrase with which coarse, narrow natures like yours think to describe experience of which you can know no more than your horse knows. It is to such as you that the good of this world falls: ready dulness, healthy selfishness, good-tempered conceit – these are the keys to happiness.'

The quick thought came, that my selfishness was even stronger than his – it was only a suffering selfishness instead of an enjoying one. But then, again, my exasperating insight into Alfred's self-complacent soul, his freedom from all the doubts and fears, the unsatisfied yearnings, the exquisite tortures of sensitiveness, that had made the web of my life, seemed to absolve me from all bonds towards him. This man needed no pity, no love; those fine influences would have been as little felt by him as the delicate white mist is felt by the rock it caresses. There was no evil in store for *him*: if he was not to marry Bertha, it would be because he had found a lot pleasanter to himself.

Mr Filmore's house lay not more than half a mile beyond our own gates, and whenever I knew my brother was gone in another direction, I went there for the chance of finding Bertha at home. Later on in the day I walked thither. By a rare accident she was alone, and we walked out in the grounds together, for she seldom went on foot beyond the trimly-swept gravel-walks. I remember what a beautiful sylph she looked to me as the low November sun shone on her blond hair, and she tripped along teasing me with her usual light banter, to which I listened half fondly, half moodily; it was all the sign Bertha's mysterious inner self ever made to me. To-day perhaps the moodiness predominated, for I had not yet shaken off the access of jealous hate which my brother had raised in me by his parting patronage. Suddenly I interrupted and startled her by saying, almost fiercely, 'Bertha, how can you love Alfred?'

She looked at me with surprise for a moment, but soon her light smile came again, and she answered sarcastically, 'Why do you suppose I love him?'

'How can you ask that, Bertha?'

'What! your wisdom thinks I must love the man I'm going to marry? The most unpleasant thing in the world. I should quarrel with him; I should be jealous of him; our *ménage*[2] would be conducted in a very ill-bred manner. A little quiet contempt contributes greatly to the elegance of life.'

'Bertha, that is not your real feeling. Why do you delight in trying to deceive me by inventing such cynical speeches?'

'I need never take the trouble of invention in order to deceive you, my small Tasso'[3] – (that was the mocking name she usually gave me). 'The easiest way to deceive a poet is to tell him the truth.'

She was testing the validity of her epigram in a daring way, and for a moment the shadow of my vision – the Bertha whose soul was no secret to me – passed between me and the radiant girl, the playful sylph whose feelings were a fascinating mystery. I suppose I must have shuddered, or betrayed in some other way my momentary chill of horror.

'Tasso !' she said, seizing my wrist, and peeping round into my face, 'are you really beginning to discern what a heartless girl I am? Why, you are not half the poet I thought you were; you are actually capable of believing the truth about me.'

The shadow passed from between us, and was no longer the object nearest to me. The girl whose light fingers grasped me, whose elfish charming face looked into mine – who, I thought, was betraying an interest in my feelings that she would not have directly avowed, – this warm-breathing presence again possessed my senses and imagination like a returning syren melody[4] which had been overpowered for an instant by the roar of threatening waves. It was a moment as delicious to me as the waking up to a consciousness of youth after a dream of middle age. I forgot everything but my passion, and said with swimming eyes –

'Bertha, shall you love me when we are first married? I wouldn't mind if you really loved me only for a little while.'

Her look of astonishment, as she loosed my hand and started away from me recalled me to a sense of my strange, my criminal indiscretion.

'Forgive me,' I said, hurriedly, as soon as I could speak again; 'I did not know what I was saying.'

'Ah, Tasso's mad fit has come on, I see,' she answered quietly, for she had recovered herself sooner than I had. 'Let him go home and keep his head cool. I must go in, for the sun is setting.'

I left her – full of indignation against myself. I had let slip words which, if she reflected on them, might rouse in her a suspicion of my abnormal mental condition – a suspicion which of all things I dreaded. And besides that, I was ashamed of the apparent baseness I had committed in uttering them to my brother's betrothed wife. I wandered home slowly, entering our park through a private gate instead of by the lodges. As I approached the house, I saw a man dashing off at full speed from the stable-yard across the park. Had any accident happened at home? No; perhaps it was only one of my father's peremptory business errands that required this headlong haste. Nevertheless I quickened my pace without any distinct motive, and was soon at the house. I will not dwell on the scene I found there. My brother was dead – had been pitched from his horse, and killed on the spot by a concussion of the brain.

I went up to the room where he lay, and where my father was seated beside him with a look of rigid despair. I had shunned my father more than any one since our return home, for the radical antipathy between our natures made my insight into his inner self a constant affliction to me. But now, as I went up to him, and stood beside him in sad silence, I felt the presence of a new element that blended us as we had never been blent before. My father had been one of the most successful men in the money-getting world: he had had no sentimental sufferings, no illness. The heaviest trouble that had befallen him was the death of his first wife. But he married my mother soon after; and I remember he seemed exactly the same, to my keen childish observation, the week after her death as before. But now, at last, a sorrow had come – the sorrow of old age, which suffers the more from the crushing of its pride and its hopes, in proportion as the pride and hope are narrow and prosaic. His son was to have been married soon – would probably have stood for the borough[5] at the next election. That son's existence was the best motive that could be alleged for making new purchases of land every year to round off the estate. It is a dreary thing to live on doing the same things year after year, without knowing why we do them. Perhaps the tragedy of disappointed youth and passion is less piteous than the tragedy of disappointed age and worldliness.

As I saw into the desolation of my father's heart, I felt a movement of deep pity towards him, which was the beginning of a new affection – an affection that grew and strengthened in spite of the strange bitterness with which he regarded me in the first month or two after my brother's death. If it had not been for the softening influence of my compassion for him – the first deep compassion I had ever felt – I should have been stung by the perception that my father transferred the inheritance of an eldest son to me with a mortified sense that fate had compelled him to the unwelcome course of caring for me as an important being. It was only in spite of himself that he began to think of me with anxious regard. There is hardly any neglected child for whom death has made vacant a more favoured place, who will not understand what I mean.

Gradually, however, my new deference to his wishes, the effect of that patience which was born of my pity for him, won upon his affection, and he began to please himself with the endeavour to make me fill my brother's place as fully as my feebler personality would admit. I saw that the prospect which by-and-by presented itself of my becoming Bertha's husband was welcome to him, and he even contemplated in my case what he had not intended in my brother's – that his son and daughter-in-law should make one household with him. My softened feeling towards my father made this the happiest time I had known since childhood; – these last months in which I retained the delicious illusion of loving Bertha, of longing and doubting and hoping that she might love me. She behaved with a certain new consciousness and distance towards me after my brother's death; and I too was under a double constraint – that of delicacy towards my brother's memory, and of anxiety as to the impression my abrupt words had left on her mind. But the additional screen this mutual reserve erected between us only brought me more completely under her power: no matter how empty the adytum, so that the veil be thick enough. So absolute is our soul's need of something hidden and uncertain for the maintenance of that doubt and hope and effort which are the breath of its life, that if the whole future were laid bare to us beyond to-day, the interest of all mankind would be bent on the hours that lie between; we should pant after the uncertainties of our one morning and our one afternoon; we should rush fiercely to the Exchange for our last possibility of speculation, of success, of disappointment; we should have a glut of political prophets foretelling a crisis or a no-crisis within the only twenty-four hours left open to prophecy. Conceive the condition of the human mind if all propositions whatsoever were self-evident except one, which was to become self-evident at the close of a summer's day, but in the meantime might be the subject of question, of hypothesis, of debate. Art and philosophy, literature and science, would fasten like bees on that one proposition which had the honey of probability in it, and be the more eager because their enjoyment would end with sunset. Our impulses, our spiritual activities, no more adjust themselves to the idea of their future nullity, than the beating of our heart, or the irritability of our muscles.

Bertha, the slim, fair-haired girl, whose present thoughts and emotions were an enigma to me amidst the fatiguing obviousness of the other minds around me, was as absorbing to me as a single unknown to-day – as a single hypothetic proposition to remain problematic till sunset; and all the cramped, hemmed-in belief and disbelief, trust and distrust, of my nature, welled out in this one narrow channel.

And she made me believe that she loved me. Without ever quitting her tone of *badinage* and playful superiority, she intoxicated me with the sense that I was necessary to her, that she was never at ease unless I was near her, submitting to her playful tyranny. It costs a woman so little effort to besot us in this way! A half-repressed word, a moment's unexpected silence, even an easy fit of petulance on our account, will serve us as *hashish*[6] for a long while. Out of the subtlest web of scarcely perceptible signs, she set me weaving the fancy that she had always unconsciously loved me better than Alfred, but that, with the ignorant fluttered sensibility of a young girl, she had been imposed on by the charm that lay for her in the distinction of being admired and chosen by a man who made so brilliant a figure in the world as my brother. She satirised herself in a very graceful way for her vanity and ambition. What was it to me that I had the light of my wretched prevision on the fact that now it was I who possessed at least all but the personal part of my brother's advantages? Our sweet illusions are half of them conscious illusions, like effects of colour that we know to be made up of tinsel, broken glass, and rags.

We were married eighteen months after Alfred's death, one cold, clear morning in April, when there came hail and sunshine both together; and Bertha, in her white silk and pale-green leaves, and the pale hues[7] of her hair and face, looked like the spirit of the morning. My father was happier than he had thought of being again: my marriage, he felt sure, would complete the desirable modification of my character, and make me practical and worldly enough to take my place in society among sane men. For he delighted in Bertha's tact and acuteness, and felt sure she would be mistress of me, and make me what she chose: I was only twenty-one, and madly in love with her. Poor father! He kept that hope a little while after our first year of marriage, and it was not quite extinct when paralysis came and saved him from utter disappointment.

I shall hurry through the rest of my story, not dwelling so much as I have hitherto done on my inward experience. When people are well known to each other, they talk rather of what befalls them externally, leaving their feelings and sentiments to be inferred.

We lived in a round of visits for some time after our return home, giving splendid dinner-parties, and making a sensation in our neighbourhood by the new lustre of our equipage, for my father had reserved this display of his increased wealth for the period of his son's marriage; and we gave our acquaintances liberal opportunity for remarking that it was a pity I made so poor a figure as an heir and a bridegroom. The nervous fatigue of this existence, the insincerities and platitudes which I had to live through twice over – through my inner and outward sense – would have been maddening to me, if I had not had that sort of intoxicated callousness which came from the delights of a first passion. A bride and bridegroom, surrounded by all the appliances of wealth, hurried through the day by the whirl of society, filling their solitary moments with hastily-snatched caresses, are prepared for their future life together as the novice is prepared for the cloister – by experiencing its utmost contrast.

Through all these crowded excited months, Bertha's inward self remained shrouded from me, and I still read her thoughts only through the language of her lips and demeanour: I had still the human interest of wondering whether what I did and said pleased her, of longing to hear a word of affection, of giving a delicious exaggeration of meaning to her smile. But I was conscious of a growing difference in her manner towards me; sometimes strong enough to be called haughty coldness, cutting and chilling me as the hail had done that came across the sunshine on our marriage morning; sometimes only perceptible in the dexterous avoidance of a *tête-à-tête* walk or dinner to which I had been looking forward. I had been deeply pained by this – had even felt a sort of crushing of the heart, from the sense that my brief day of happiness was near its setting; but still I remained dependent on Bertha, eager for the last rays of a bliss that would soon be gone for ever, hoping and watching for some after-glow more beautiful from the impending night.

I remember – how should I not remember? – the time when that dependence and hope utterly left me, when the sadness I had felt in Bertha's growing estrangement became a joy that I looked back upon with longing, as a man might look back on the last pains in a paralysed limb. It was just after the close of my father's last illness, which had necessarily withdrawn us from society and thrown us more upon each other. It was the evening of my father's death. On that evening the veil which had shrouded Bertha's soul from me – had made me find in her alone among my fellow-beings the blessed possibility of mystery, and doubt, and expectation – was first withdrawn. Perhaps it was the first day since the beginning of my passion for her, in which that passion was completely neutralised by the presence of an absorbing feeling of another kind. I had been watching by my father's deathbed: I had been witnessing the last fitful yearning glance his soul had cast back on the spent inheritance of life – the last faint consciousness of love he had gathered from the pressure of my hand. What are all our personal loves when we have been sharing in that supreme agony? In the first moments when we come away from the presence of death, every other relation to the living is merged, to our feeling, in the great relation of a common nature and a common destiny.

In that state of mind I joined Bertha in her private sitting-room. She was seated in a leaning posture on a settee, with her back towards the door; the great rich coils of her pale blond hair surmounting her small neck, visible above the back of the settee. I remember, as I closed the door behind me, a cold tremulousness seizing me, and a vague sense of being hated and lonely – vague and strong, like a presentiment. I know how I looked at that moment, for I saw myself in Bertha's thought as she lifted her cutting grey eyes, and looked at me: a miserable ghost-seer, surrounded by phantoms in the noonday, trembling under a breeze when the leaves were still, without appetite for the common objects of human desire, but pining after the moonbeams. We were front to front with each other, and judged each other. The terrible moment of complete illumination had come to me, and I saw that the darkness had hidden no landscape from me, but only a blank prosaic wall: from that evening forth, through the sickening years which followed, I saw all round the narrow room of this woman's soul – saw petty artifice and mere negation where I had delighted to believe in coy sensibilities and in wit at war with latent feeling – saw the light floating vanities of the girl defining themselves into the systematic coquetry, the scheming selfish-ness, of the woman – saw repulsion and antipathy harden into cruel hatred, giving pain only for the sake of wreaking itself.

For Bertha too, after her kind, felt the bitterness of disillusion. She had believed that my wild poet's passion for her would make me her slave; and that, being her slave, I should execute her will in all things. With the essential shallowness of a negative, unimaginative nature, she was unable to conceive the fact that sensibilities were anything else than weaknesses. She had thought my weaknesses would put me in her power, and she found them unmanageable forces. Our positions were reversed. Before marriage she had completely mastered my imagina-tion, for she was a secret to me; and I created the unknown thought before which I trembled as if it were hers. But now that her soul was laid open to me, now that I was compelled to share the privacy of her motives, to follow all the petty devices that preceded her words and acts, she found herself powerless with me, except to produce in me the chill shudder of repulsion – powerless, because I could be acted on by no lever within her reach. I was dead to worldly ambitions, to social vanities, to all the incentives within the compass of her narrow imagina-tion, and I lived under influences utterly invisible to her.

She was really pitiable to have such a husband, and so all the world thought. A graceful, brilliant woman, like Bertha, who smiled on morning callers, made a figure in ball-rooms, and was capable of that light repartee which, from such a woman, is accepted as wit, was secure of carrying off all sympathy from a husband who was sickly, abstracted, and, as some suspected, crack-brained.[8] Even the servants in our house gave her the balance of their regard and pity. For there were no audible quarrels between us; our alienation, our repulsion from each other, lay within the silence of our own hearts; and if the mistress went out a great deal, and seemed to dislike the master's society, was it not natural, poor thing? The master was odd. I was kind and just to my dependants, but I excited in them a shrinking, half-contemptuous pity; for this class of men and women are but slightly determined in their estimate of others by general considerations, or even experience, of character. They judge of persons as they judge of coins, and value those who pass current at a high rate.

After a time I interfered so little with Bertha's habits, that it might seem wonderful how her hatred towards me could grow so intense and active as it did. But she had begun to suspect, by some involuntary betrayals of mine, that there was an abnormal power of penetration in me – that fitfully, at least, I was strangely cognisant of her thoughts and intentions, and she began to be haunted by a terror of me, which alternated every now and then with defiance. She meditated continually how the incubus[9] could be shaken off her life – how she could be freed from this hateful bond to a being whom she at once despised as an imbecile, and dreaded as an inquisitor. For a long while she lived in the hope that my evident wretchedness would drive me to the commission of suicide; but suicide was not in my nature. I was too completely swayed by the sense that I was in the grasp of unknown forces, to believe in my power of self-release. Towards my own destiny I had become entirely passive; for my one ardent desire had spent itself, and impulse no longer predominated over knowledge. For this reason I never thought of taking any steps towards a complete separation, which would have made our alienation evident to the world. Why should I rush for help to a new course, when I was only suffering from the consequences of a deed which had been the act of my intensest will? That would have been the logic of one who had desires to gratify, and I had no desires. But Bertha and I lived more and more aloof from each other. The rich find it easy to live married and apart.

That course of our life which I have indicated in a few sentences filled the space of years. So much misery – so slow and hideous a growth of hatred and sin, may be compressed into a sentence! And men judge of each other's lives through this summary medium. They epitomise the experience of their fellow-mortal, and pronounce judgment on him in neat syntax, and feel themselves wise and virtuous – conquerors over the temptations they define in well-selected predicates. Seven years of wretchedness glide glibly over the lips of the man who has never counted them out in moments of chill disappointment, of head and heart throbbings, of dread and vain wrestling, of remorse and despair. We learn *words* by rote,[10] but not their meaning; *that* must be paid for with our life-blood, and printed in the subtle fibres of our nerves.

But I will hasten to finish my story. Brevity is justified at once to those who readily understand, and to those who will never understand.

Some years after my father's death, I was sitting by the dim firelight in my library one January evening – sitting in the leather chair that used to be my father's – when Bertha appeared at the door, with a candle in her hand, and advanced towards me. I knew the ball-dress she had on – the white ball-dress, with the green jewels, shone upon by the light of the wax candle which lit up the medallion of the dying Cleopatra on the mantelpiece. Why did she come to me before going out? I had not seen her in the library, which was my habitual place, for months. Why did she stand before me with the candle in her hand, with her cruel contemptuous eyes fixed on me, and the glittering serpent, like a familiar demon,[11] on her breast? For a moment I thought this fulfilment of my vision at Vienna marked some dreadful crisis in my fate, but I saw nothing in Bertha's mind, as she stood before me, except scorn for the look of overwhelming misery with which I sat before her ... 'Fool, idiot, why don't you kill yourself, then?' – that was her thought. But at length her thoughts reverted to her errand, and she spoke aloud. The apparently indifferent nature of the errand seemed to make a ridiculous anticlimax to my prevision and my agitation.

'I have had to hire a new maid. Fletcher is going to be married, and she wants me to ask you to let her husband have the public-house and farm at Molton. I wish him to have it. You must give the promise now, because Fletcher is going to-morrow morning – and quickly, because I'm in a hurry.'

'Very well; you may promise her,' I said, indifferently, and Bertha swept out of the library again.

I always shrank from the sight of a new person, and all the more when it was a person whose mental life was likely to weary my reluctant insight with worldly ignorant trivialities. But I shrank especially from the sight of this new maid, because her advent had been announced to me at a moment to which I could not cease to attach some fatality: I had a vague dread that I should find her mixed up with the dreary drama of my life – that some new sickening vision would reveal her to me as an evil genius. When at last I did unavoidably meet her, the vague dread was changed into definite disgust. She was a tall, wiry, dark-eyed woman, this Mrs Archer, with a face handsome enough to give her coarse hard nature the odious finish of bold, self-confident coquetry. That was enough to make me avoid her, quite apart from the contemptuous feeling with which she contemplated me. I seldom saw her; but I perceived that she rapidly became a favourite with her mistress, and, after the lapse of eight or nine months, I began to be aware that there had arisen in Bertha's mind towards this woman a mingled feeling of fear and dependence, and that this feeling was associated with ill-defined images of candle-light scenes in her dressing-room, and the looking-up of something in Bertha's cabinet. My interviews with my wife had become so brief and so rarely solitary, that I had no opportunity of perceiving these images in her mind with more definiteness. The recollections of the past become contracted in the rapidity of thought till they sometimes bear hardly a more distinct resemblance to the external reality than the forms of an oriental alphabet to the objects that suggested them.

Besides, for the last year or more a modification had been going forward in my mental condition, and was growing more and more marked. My insight into the minds of those around me was becoming dimmer and more fitful, and the ideas that crowded my double consciousness became less and less dependent on any personal contact. All that was personal in me seemed to be suffering a gradual death, so that I was losing the organ through which the personal agitations and projects of others could affect me. But along with this relief from wearisome insight, there was a new development of what I concluded – as I have since found rightly – to be a prevision of external scenes. It was as if the relation between me and my fellow-men was more and more deadened, and my relation to what we call the inanimate was quickened into new life. The more I lived apart from society, and in proportion as my wretchedness subsided from the violent throb of agonised passion into the dulness of habitual pain, the more frequent and vivid became such visions as that I had had of Prague – of strange cities, of sandy plains, of gigantic ruins, of midnight skies with strange bright constellations, of mountain-passes, of grassy nooks flecked with the afternoon sunshine through the boughs: I was in the midst of such scenes, and in all of them one presence seemed to weigh on me in all these mighty shapes – the presence of something unknown and pitiless. For continual suffering had annihilated religious faith within me: to the utterly miserable – the unloving and the unloved – there is no religion possible, no worship but a worship of devils. And beyond all these, and continually recurring, was the vision of my death – the pangs, the suffocation, the last struggle, when life would be grasped at in vain.

Things were in this state near the end of the seventh year. I had become entirely free from insight, from my abnormal cognisance of any other consciousness than my own, and instead of intruding involuntarily into the world of other minds, was living continually in my own solitary future. Bertha was aware that I was greatly changed. To my surprise she had of late seemed to seek opportunities of remaining in my society, and had cultivated that kind of distant yet familiar talk which is customary between a husband and wife who live in polite and irrevocable alienation. I bore this with languid submission, and without feeling enough interest in her motives to be roused into keen observation; yet I could not help perceiving something triumphant and excited in her carriage and the expression of her face – something too subtle to express itself in words or tones, but giving one the idea that she lived in a state of expectation or hopeful suspense. My chief feeling was satisfaction that her inner self was once more shut out from me; and I almost revelled for the moment in the absent melancholy that made me answer her at cross purposes, and betray utter ignorance of what she had been saying. I remember well the look and the smile with which she one day said, after a mistake of this kind on my part: 'I used to think you were a clairvoyant[12] and that was the reason why you were so bitter against other clairvoyants, wanting to keep your monopoly; but I see now you have become rather duller than the rest of the world.'

I said nothing in reply. It occurred to me that her recent obtrusion of herself upon me might have been prompted by the wish to test my power of detecting some of her secrets; but I let the thought drop again at once: her motives and her deeds had no interest for me, and whatever pleasures she might be seeking, I had no wish to balk her. There was still pity in my soul for every living thing, and Bertha was living – was surrounded with possibilities of misery.

Just at this time there occurred an event which roused me somewhat from my inertia, and gave me an interest in the passing moment that I had thought impossible for me. It was a visit from Charles Meunier, who had written me word that he was coming to England for relaxation from too strenuous labour, and would like to see me. Meunier had now a European reputation; but his letter to me expressed that keen remembrance of an early regard, an early debt of sympathy, which is inseparable from nobility of character: and I too felt as if his presence would be to me like a transient resurrection into a happier pre-existence.

He came, and as far as possible, I renewed our old pleasure of making *tête-à-tête* excursions, though, instead of mountains and glaciers and the wide blue lake, we had to content ourselves with mere slopes and ponds and artificial plantations. The years had changed us both, but with what different result! Meunier was now a brilliant figure in society, to whom elegant women pretended to listen, and whose acquaintance was boasted of by noblemen ambitious of brains. He repressed with the utmost delicacy all betrayal of the shock which I am sure he must have received from our meeting, or of a desire to penetrate into my condition and circumstances, and sought by the utmost exertion of his charming social powers to make our reunion agreeable. Bertha was much struck by the unexpected fascinations of a visitor whom she had expected to find presentable only on the score of his celebrity, and put forth all her coquetries and accomplishments. Apparently she succeeded in attracting his admiration, for his manner towards her was attentive and flattering. The effect of his presence on me was so benignant, especially in those renewals of our old *tête-à-tête* wanderings, when he poured forth to me wonderful narratives of his professional experience, that more than once, when his talk turned on the psychological relations of disease, the thought crossed my mind that, if his stay with me were long enough, I might possibly bring myself to tell this man the secrets of my lot. Might there not lie some remedy for *me*, too, in his science? Might there not at least lie some comprehension and sympathy ready for me in his large and susceptible mind? But the thought only flickered feebly now and then, and died out before it could become a wish. The horror I had of again breaking in on the privacy of another soul, made me, by an irrational instinct, draw the shroud of concealment more closely around my own, as we automatically perform the gesture we feel to be wanting in another.

When Meunier's visit was approaching its conclusion, there happened an event which caused some excitement in our household, owing to the surprisingly strong effect it appeared to produce on Bertha – on Bertha, the self-possessed, who usually seemed inaccessible to feminine agitations, and did even her hate in a self-restrained hygienic manner. This event was the sudden severe illness of her maid, Mrs Archer. I have reserved to this moment the mention of a circumstance which had forced itself on my notice shortly before Meunier's arrival, namely, that there had been some quarrel between Bertha and this maid, apparently during a visit to a distant family, in which she had accompanied her mistress. I had overheard Archer speaking in a tone of bitter insolence, which I should have thought an adequate reason for immediate dismissal. No dismissal followed; on the contrary, Bertha seemed to be silently putting up with personal inconveniences from the exhibitions of this woman's temper. I was the more astonished to observe that her illness seemed a cause of strong solicitude to Bertha; that she was at the bedside night and day, and would allow no one else to officiate as head-nurse. It happened that our family doctor was out on a holiday, an accident which made Meunier's presence in the house doubly welcome, and he apparently entered into the case with an interest which seemed so much stronger than the ordinary professional feeling, that one day when he had fallen into a long fit of silence after visiting her, I said to him –

'Is this a very peculiar case of disease, Meunier?'

'No,' he answered, 'it is an attack of peritonitis,[13] which will be fatal, but which does not differ physically from many other cases that have come under my observation. But I'll tell you what I have on my mind. I want to make an experiment on this woman, if you will give me permission. It can do her no harm – will give her no pain – for I shall not make it until life is extinct to all purposes of sensation. I want to try the effect of transfusing blood[14] into her arteries after the heart has ceased to beat for some minutes. I have tried the experiment again and again with animals that have died of this disease, with astounding results, and I want to try it on a human subject. I have the small tubes necessary, in a case I have with me, and the rest of the apparatus could be prepared readily. I should use my own blood – take it from my own arm. This woman won't live through the night, I'm convinced, and I want you to promise me your assistance in making the experiment. I can't do without another hand, but it would perhaps not be well to call in a medical assistant from among your provincial doctors. A disagreeable foolish version of the thing might get abroad.'

'Have you spoken to my wife on the subject?' I said, 'because she appears to be peculiarly sensitive about this woman: she has been a favourite maid.'

'To tell you the truth,' said Meunier, 'I don't want her to know about it. There are always insuperable difficulties with women in these matters, and the effect on the supposed dead body may be startling. You and I will sit up together, and be in readiness. When certain symptoms appear I shall take you in, and at the right moment we must manage to get every one else out of the room.'

I need not give our farther conversation on the subject. He entered very fully into the details, and overcame my repulsion from them, by exciting in me a mingled awe and curiosity concerning the possible results of his experiment.

We prepared everything, and he instructed me in my part as assistant. He had not told Bertha of his absolute conviction that Archer would not survive through the night, and endeavoured to persuade her to leave the patient and take a night's rest. But she was obstinate, suspecting the fact that death was at hand, and supposing that he wished merely to save her nerves. She refused to leave the sick-room. Meunier and I sat up together in the library, he making frequent visits to the sick-room, and returning with the information that the case was taking precisely the course he expected. Once he said to me, 'Can you imagine any cause of ill feeling this woman has against her mistress, who is so devoted to her?'

'I think there was some misunderstanding between them before her illness. Why do you ask?'

'Because I have observed for the last five or six hours – since, I fancy, she has lost all hope of recovery – there seems a strange prompting in her to say something which pain and failing strength forbid her to utter; and there is a look of hideous meaning in her eyes, which she turns continually towards her mistress. In this disease the mind often remains singularly clear to the last.'

'I am not surprised at an indication of malevolent feeling in her,' I said. 'She is a woman who has always inspired me with distrust and dislike, but she managed to insinuate herself into her mistress's favour.' He was silent after this, looking at the fire with an air of absorption, till he went up-stairs again. He stayed away longer than usual, and on returning, said to me quietly, 'Come now.'

I followed him to the chamber where death was hovering. The dark hangings of the large bed made a background that gave a strong relief to Bertha's pale face as I entered. She started forward as she saw me enter, and then looked at Meunier with an expression of angry inquiry; but he lifted up his hand as if to impose silence, while he fixed his glance on the dying woman and felt her pulse. The face was pinched and ghastly, a cold perspiration was on the forehead, and the eyelids were lowered so as almost to conceal the large dark eyes. After a minute or two, Meunier walked round to the other side of the bed where Bertha stood, and with his usual air of gentle politeness towards her begged her to leave the patient under our care – everything should be done for her – she was no longer in a state to be conscious of an affectionate presence. Bertha was hesitating, apparently almost willing to believe his assurance and to comply. She looked round at the ghastly dying face, as if to read the confirmation of that assurance, when for a moment the lowered eyelids were raised again, and it seemed as if the eyes were looking towards Bertha, but blankly. A shudder passed through Bertha's frame, and she returned to her station near the pillow, tacitly implying that she would not leave the room.

The eyelids were lifted no more. Once I looked at Bertha as she watched the face of the dying one. She wore a rich *peignoir*,[15] and her blond hair was half covered by a lace cap: in her attire she was, as always, an elegant woman, fit to figure in a picture of modern aristocratic life: but I asked myself how that face of hers could ever have seemed to me the face of a woman born of woman, with memories of childhood, capable of pain, needing to be fondled? The features at that moment seemed so preternaturally sharp, the eyes were so hard and eager – she looked like a cruel immortal, finding her spiritual feast in the agonies of a dying race. For across those hard features there came something like a flash when the last hour had been breathed out, and we all felt that the dark veil had completely fallen. What secret was there between Bertha and this woman? I turned my eyes from her with a horrible dread lest my insight should return, and I should be obliged to see what had been breeding about two unloving women's hearts. I felt that Bertha had been watching for the moment of death as the sealing of her secret: I thanked Heaven it could remain sealed for me.

Meunier said quietly, 'She is gone.' He then gave his arm to Bertha, and she submitted to be led out of the room.

I suppose it was at her order that two female attendants came into the room, and dismissed the younger one who had been present before. When they entered, Meunier had already opened the artery in the long thin neck that lay rigid on the pillow, and I dismissed them, ordering them to remain at a distance till we rang: the doctor, I said, had an operation to perform – he was not sure about the death. For the next twenty minutes I forgot everything but Meunier and the experiment in which he was so absorbed, that I think his senses would have been closed against all sounds or sights which had no relation to it. It was my task at first to keep up the artificial respiration[16] in the body after the transfusion had been effected, but presently Meunier relieved me, and I could see the wondrous slow return of life; the breast began to heave, the inspirations became stronger, the eyelids quivered, and the soul seemed to have returned beneath them. The artificial respiration was withdrawn: still the breathing continued, and there was a movement of the lips.

Just then I heard the handle of the door moving: I suppose Bertha had heard from the women that they had been dismissed: probably a vague fear had arisen in her mind, for she entered with a look of alarm. She came to the foot of the bed and gave a stifled cry.

The dead woman's eyes were wide open, and met hers in full recognition – the recognition of hate. With a sudden strong effort, the hand that Bertha had thought for ever still was pointed towards her, and the haggard face moved. The gasping eager voice said –

'You mean to poison your husband ... the poison is in the black cabinet ... I got it for you ... you laughed at me, and told lies about me behind my back, to make me disgusting ... because you were jealous ... are you sorry ... now?'

The lips continued to murmur, but the sounds were no longer distinct. Soon there was no sound – only a slight movement: the flame had leaped out, and was being extinguished the faster. The wretched woman's heart-strings had been set to hatred and vengeance; the spirit of life had swept the chords for an instant, and was gone again for ever. Great God! Is this what it is to live again[17] ... to wake up with our unstilled thirst upon us, with our unuttered curses rising to our lips, with our muscles ready to act out their half-committed sins?

Bertha stood pale at the foot of the bed, quivering and helpless, despairing of devices, like a cunning animal whose hiding-places are surrounded by swift-advancing flame. Even Meunier looked paralysed; life for that moment ceased to be a scientific problem to him. As for me, this scene seemed of one texture with the rest of my existence: horror was my familiar, and this new revelation was only like an old pain recurring with new circumstances.

Since then Bertha and I have lived apart – she in her own neighbour-hood, the mistress of half our wealth, I as a wanderer in foreign countries, until I came to this Devonshire nest to die. Bertha lives pitied and admired; for what had I against that charming woman, whom every one but myself could have been happy with? There had been no witness of the scene in the dying room except Meunier, and while Meunier lived his lips were sealed by a promise to me.

Once or twice, weary of wandering, I rested in a favourite spot, and my heart went out towards the men and women and children whose faces were becoming familiar to me: but I was driven away again in terror at the approach of my old insight – driven away to live continu-ally with the one Unknown Presence revealed and yet hidden by the moving curtain of the earth and sky. Till at last disease took hold of me and forced me to rest here – forced me to live in dependence on my servants. And then the curse of insight – of my double conscious-ness, came again, and has never left me. I know all their narrow thoughts, their feeble regard, their half-wearied pity.

It is the 20th of September 1850. I know these figures I have just written, as if they were a long familiar inscription. I have seen them on this page in my desk unnumbered times, when the scene of my dying struggle has opened upon me. ...

(1859.)

Brother Jacob

'Trompeurs, c'est pour vous que j'écris,
Attendez vous à la pareille.'[1]

— LA FONTAINE.

CHAPTER I

Among the many fatalities attending the bloom of young desire, that of blindly taking to the confectionery line has not, perhaps, been sufficiently considered. How is the son of a British yeoman,[1] who has been fed principally on salt pork and yeast dumplings, to know that there is satiety for the human stomach even in a paradise of glass jars full of sugared almonds and pink lozenges, and that the tedium of life can reach a pitch where plum-buns at discretion cease to offer the slightest enticement? Or how, at the tender age when a confectioner[2] seems to him a very prince whom all the world must envy, – who breakfasts on macaroons, dines on marengs, sups on twelfth-cake,[3] and fills up the intermediate hours with sugar-candy or peppermint, – how is he to foresee the day of sad wisdom, when he will discern that the confectioner's calling is not socially influential, or favourable to a soaring ambition? I have known a man who turned out to have a metaphysical genius, incautiously, in the period of youthful buoyancy, commence his career as a dancing-master; and you may imagine the use that was made of this initial mistake by opponents who felt themselves bound to warn the public against his doctrine of the Inconceivable.[4] He could not give up his dancing-lessons, because he made his bread by them, and metaphysics would not have found him in so much as salt to his bread. It was really the same with Mr David Faux and the confectionery business. His uncle, the butler at the great house close by Brigford, had made a pet of him in his early boyhood, and it was on a visit to this uncle that the confectioners' shops in that brilliant town had, on a single day, fired his tender imagination. He carried home the pleasing illusion that a confectioner must be at once the happiest and the foremost of men, since the things he made were not only the most beautiful to behold, but the very best eating, and such as the Lord Mayor must always order largely for his private recreation; so that when his father declared he must be put to a trade, David chose his line without a moment's hesitation; and, with a rashness inspired by a sweet tooth, wedded himself irrevocably to confectionery. Soon, however, the tooth lost its relish and fell into blank indifference; and all the while, his mind expanded, his ambition took new shapes, which could hardly be satisfied within the sphere his youthful ardour had chosen. But what was he to do? He was a young man of much mental activity, and, above all, gifted with a spirit of contrivance; but then, his faculties would not tell with great effect in any other medium than that of candied sugars, conserves, and pastry. Say what you will about the identity of the reasoning process in all branches of thought, or about the advantage of coming to subjects with a fresh mind, the adjustment of butter to flour, and of heat to pastry, is *not* the best preparation for the office of prime minister; besides, in the present imperfectly-organised state of society, there are social barriers. David could invent delightful things in the way of drop-cakes, and he had the widest views of the sugar department;[5] but in other directions he certainly felt hampered by the want of knowledge and practical skill; and the world is so inconveniently constituted, that the vague consciousness of being a fine fellow is no guarantee of success in any line of business.

This difficulty pressed with some severity on Mr David Faux, even before his apprenticeship was ended. His soul swelled with an impatient sense that he ought to become something very remarkable – that it was quite out of the question for him to put up with a narrow lot as other men did: he scorned the idea that he could accept an average. He was sure there was nothing average about him; even such a person as Mrs Tibbits, the washerwoman, perceived it, and probably had a preference for his linen. At that particular period he was weighing out gingerbread-nuts; but such an anomaly could not continue. No position could be suited to Mr David Faux that was not in the highest degree easy to the flesh and flattering to the spirit. If he had fallen on the present times, and enjoyed the advantages of a Mechanics' Institute,[6] he would certainly have taken to literature and have written reviews; but his education had not been liberal. He had read some novels from the adjoining circulating library, and had even bought the story of 'Inkle and Yarico,'[7] which had made him feel very sorry for poor Mr Inkle; so that his ideas might not have been below a certain mark[8] of the literary calling; but his spelling and diction were too unconventional.

When a man is not adequately appreciated or comfortably placed in his own country, his thoughts naturally turn towards foreign climes; and David's imagination circled round and round the utmost limits of his geographical knowledge, in search of a country where a young gentleman of pasty visage, lipless mouth, and stumpy hair, would be likely to be received with the hospitable enthusiasm which he had a right to expect. Having a general idea of America as a country where the population was chiefly black, it appeared to him the most propitious destination for an emigrant who, to begin with, had the broad and easily recognisable merit of whiteness; and this idea gradually took such strong possession of him that Satan seized the opportunity of suggesting to him that he might emigrate under easier circumstances, if he supplied himself with a little money from his master's till. But that evil spirit, whose understanding, I am convinced, has been much overrated, quite wasted his time on this occasion. David would certainly have liked well to have some of his master's money in his pocket, if he had been sure his master would have been the only man to suffer for it; but he was a cautious youth, and quite determined to run no risks on his own account. So he stayed out his apprenticeship, and committed no act of dishonesty that was at all likely to be discovered, reserving his plan of emigration for a future opportunity. And the circumstances under which he carried it out were in this wise. Having been at home a week or two partaking of the family beans,[9] he had used his leisure in ascertaining a fact which was of considerable importance to him, namely, that his mother had a small sum in guineas painfully saved from her maiden perquisites, and kept in the corner of a drawer where her baby-linen had reposed for the last twenty years – ever since her son David had taken to his feet, with a slight promise of bow-legs which had not been altogether unfulfilled. Mr Faux, senior, had told his son very frankly, that he must not look to being set-up in business by *him:* with seven sons, and one of them a very healthy and well-developed idiot, who consumed a dumpling about eight inches in diameter every day, it was pretty well if they got a hundred apiece at his death. Under these circumstances, what was David to do? It was certainly hard that he should take his mother's money; but he saw no other ready means of getting any, and it was not to be expected that a young man of his merit should put up with inconveniences that could be avoided. Besides, it is not robbery to take property belonging to your mother: she doesn't prosecute you. And David was very well behaved to his mother; he comforted her by speaking highly of himself to her, and assuring her that he never fell into the vices he saw practised by other youths of his own age, and that he was particularly fond of honesty. If his mother would have given him her twenty guineas as a reward of this noble disposition, he really would not have stolen them from her, and it would have been more agreeable to his feelings. Nevertheless, to an active mind like David's, ingenuity is not without its pleasures: it was rather an interesting occupation to become stealthily acquainted with the wards of his mother's simple key (not in the least like Chubb's patent),[10] and to get one that would do its work equally well; and also to arrange a little drama by which he would escape suspicion, and run no risk of forfeiting the prospective hundred at his father's death, which would be convenient in the improbable case of his *not* making a large fortune in the 'Indies.'

First, he spoke freely of his intention to start shortly for Liverpool and take ship for America; a resolution which cost his good mother some pain, for, after Jacob the idiot, there was not one of her sons to whom her heart clung more than to her youngest-born, David. Next, it appeared to him that Sunday afternoon, when everybody was gone to church except Jacob and the cow-boy, was so singularly favourable an opportunity for sons who wanted to appropriate their mothers' guineas, that he half thought it must have been kindly intended by Providence for such purposes. Especially the third Sunday in Lent; because Jacob had been out on one of his occasional wanderings for the last two days; and David, being a timid young man, had a considerable dread and hatred of Jacob, as of a large personage who went about habitually with a pitchfork in his hand.

Nothing could be easier, then, than for David on this Sunday afternoon to decline going to church, on the ground that he was going to tea at Mr Lunn's, whose pretty daughter Sally[11] had been an early flame of his, and, when the church-goers were at a safe distance, to abstract the guineas from their wooden box and slip them into a small canvas bag – nothing easier than to call to the cow-boy that he was going, and tell him to keep an eye on the house for fear of Sunday tramps. David thought it would be easy, too, to get to a small thicket and bury his bag in a hole he had already made and covered up under the roots of an old hollow ash, and he had, in fact, found the hole without a moment's difficulty, had uncovered it, and was about gently to drop the bag into it, when the sound of a large body rustling towards him with something like a bellow was such a surprise to David, who, as a gentleman gifted with much contrivance, was naturally only prepared for what he expected, that instead of dropping the bag gently he let it fall so as to make it untwist and vomit forth the shining guineas. In the same moment he looked up and saw his dear brother Jacob close upon him, holding the pitchfork so that the bright smooth prongs were a yard in advance of his own body, and about a foot off David's. (A learned friend, to whom I once narrated this history, observed that it was David's guilt which made these prongs formidable, and that the *mens nil conscia sibi*[12] strips a pitchfork of all terrors. I thought this idea so valuable, that I obtained his leave to use it on condition of suppressing his name.) Nevertheless, David did not entirely lose his presence of mind; for in that case he would have sunk on the earth or started backward; whereas he kept his ground and smiled at Jacob, who nodded his head up and down, and said, 'Hoich, Zavy!' in a painfully equivocal manner. David's heart was beating audibly, and if he had had any lips they would have been pale; but his mental activity, instead of being paralysed, was stimulated. While he was inwardly praying (he always prayed when he was much frightened), – 'Oh, save me this once, and I'll never get into danger again!'– he was thrusting his hand into his pocket in search of a box of yellow lozenges, which he had brought with him from Brigford among other delicacies of the same portable kind, as a means of conciliating proud beauty, and more particularly the beauty of Miss Sarah Lunn. Not one of these delicacies had he ever offered to poor Jacob, for David was not a young man to waste his jujubes [13] and barley-sugar in giving pleasure to people from whom he expected nothing. But an idiot with equivocal intentions and a pitchfork is as well worth flattering and cajoling as if he were Louis Napoleon.[14] So David, with a promptitude equal to the occasion, drew out his box of yellow lozenges, lifted the lid, and performed a pantomime with his mouth and fingers, which was meant to imply that he was delighted to see his dear brother Jacob, and seized the opportunity of making him a small present, which he would find particularly agreeable to the taste. Jacob, you understand, was not an intense idiot, but within a certain limited range knew how to choose the good and reject the evil: he took one lozenge, by way of test, and sucked it as if he had been a philosopher; then, in as great an ecstasy at its new and complex savour as Caliban at the taste of Trinculo's wine,[15] chuckled and stroked this suddenly beneficent brother, and held out his hand for more; for, except in fits of anger, Jacob was not ferocious or needlessly predatory. David's courage half returned, and he left off praying; pouring a dozen lozenges into Jacob's palm, and trying to look very fond of him. He congratulated himself that he had formed the plan of going to see Miss Sally Lunn this afternoon, and that, as a consequence, he had brought with him these propitiatory delicacies: he was certainly a lucky fellow; indeed, it was always likely Providence should be fonder of him than of other apprentices, and since he *was* to be interrupted, why, an idiot was preferable to any other sort of witness. For the first time in his life, David thought he saw the advantage of idiots.

As for Jacob, he had thrust his pitchfork into the ground, and had thrown himself down beside it, in thorough abandonment to the unprecedented pleasure of having five lozenges in his mouth at once, blinking meanwhile, and making inarticulate sounds of gustative content. He had not yet given any sign of noticing the guineas, but in seating himself he had laid his broad right hand on them, and unconsciously kept it in that position, absorbed in the sensations of his palate. If he could only be kept so occupied with the lozenges as not to see the guineas before David could manage to cover them!

That was David's best hope of safety; for Jacob knew his mother's guineas; it had been part of their common experience as boys to be allowed to look at these handsome coins, and rattle them in their box on high days and holidays, and among all Jacob's narrow experiences as to money, this was likely to be the most memorable.

'Here, Jacob,' said David, in an insinuating tone, handing the box to him, 'I'll give 'em all to you. Run! – make haste! – else somebody'll come and take 'em.'

David, not having studied the psychology of idiots,[16] was not aware that they are not to be wrought upon by imaginative fears. Jacob took the box with his left hand, but saw no necessity for running away. Was ever a promising young man wishing to lay the foundation of his fortune by appropriating his mother's guineas obstructed by such a day-mare[17] as this? But the moment must come when Jacob would move his right hand to draw off the lid of the tin box, and then David would sweep the guineas into the hole with the utmost address and swiftness, and immediately seat himself upon them. Ah, no! It's of no use to have foresight when you are dealing with an idiot: he is not to be calculated upon. Jacob's right hand was given to vague clutching and throwing; it suddenly clutched the guineas as if they had been so many pebbles, and was raised in an attitude which promised to scatter them like seed over a distant bramble, when, from some prompting or other – probably of an unwonted sensation – it paused, descended to Jacob's knee, and opened slowly under the inspection of Jacob's dull eyes. David began to pray again, but immediately desisted – another resource having occurred to him.

'Mother! zinnies!' exclaimed the innocent Jacob. Then, looking at David, he said, interrogatively, 'Box?'

'Hush! hush!' said David, summoning all his ingenuity in this severe strait. ' See, Jacob!' He took the tin box from his brother's hand, and emptied it of the lozenges, returning half of them to Jacob, but secretly keeping the rest in his own hand. Then he held out the empty box, and said, 'Here's the box, Jacob! The box for the guineas!' gently sweeping them from Jacob's palm into the box.

This procedure was not objectionable to Jacob; on the contrary, the guineas clinked so pleasantly as they fell, that he wished for a repetition of the sound, and seizing the box, began to rattle it very gleefully. David, seizing the opportunity, deposited his reserve of lozenges in the ground and hastily swept some earth over them. 'Look, Jacob!' he said, at last. Jacob paused from his clinking, and looked into the hole, while David began to scratch away the earth, as if in doubtful expectation. When the lozenges were laid bare, he took them out one by one, and gave them to Jacob.

'Hush!' he said, in a loud whisper, 'Tell nobody – all for Jacob – hush – sh – sh! Put guineas in the hole – they'll come out like this!' To make the lesson more complete, he took a guinea, and lowering it into the hole, said, 'Put in *so*.' Then, as he took the last lozenge out, he said, 'Come out *so*,' and put the lozenge into Jacob's hospitable mouth.

Jacob turned his head on one side, looked first at his brother and then at the hole, like a reflective monkey, and, finally, laid the box of guineas in the hole with much decision. David made haste to add every one of the stray coins, put on the lid, and covered it well with earth, saying in his most coaxing tone –

'Take 'm out to-morrow, Jacob; all for Jacob! Hush – sh – sh!'

Jacob, to whom this once indifferent brother had all at once become a sort of sweet-tasted fetish,[18] stroked David's best coat with his adhesive fingers, and then hugged him with an accompaniment of that mingled chuckling and gurgling by which he was accustomed to express the milder passions. But if he had chosen to bite a small morsel out of his beneficent brother's cheek, David would have been obliged to bear it.

And here I must pause, to point out to you the short-sightedness of human contrivance. This ingenious young man, Mr David Faux, thought he had achieved a triumph of cunning when he had associated himself in his brother's rudimentary mind with the flavour of yellow lozenges. But he had yet to learn that it is a dreadful thing to make an idiot fond of you, when you yourself are not of an affectionate disposition: especially an idiot with a pitchfork – obviously a difficult friend to shake off by rough usage.

It may seem to you rather a blundering contrivance for a clever young man to bury the guineas. But, if everything had turned out as David had calculated, you would have seen that his plan was worthy of his talents. The guineas would have lain safely in the earth while the theft was discovered, and David, with the calm of conscious innocence, would have lingered at home, reluctant to say good-bye to his dear mother while she was in grief about her guineas; till at length, on the eve of his departure, he would have disinterred them in the strictest privacy, and carried them on his own person without inconvenience. But David, you perceive, had reckoned without his host,[19] or, to speak more precisely, without his idiot brother – an item of so uncertain and fluctuating a character, that I doubt whether he would not have puzzled the astute heroes of M. de Balzac,[20] whose foresight is so remarkably at home in the future.

It was clear to David now that he had only one alternative before him: he must either renounce the guineas, by quietly putting them back in his mother's drawer (a course not unattended with difficulty); or he must leave more than a suspicion behind him, by departing early the next morning without giving notice, and with the guineas in his pocket. For if he gave notice that he was going, his mother, he knew, would insist on fetching from her box of guineas the three she had always promised him as his share; indeed, in his original plan, he had counted on this as a means by which the theft would be discovered under circumstances that would themselves speak for his innocence; but now, as I need hardly explain, that well-combined plan was completely frustrated. Even if David could have bribed Jacob with perpetual lozenges, an idiot's secrecy is itself betrayal. He dared not even go to tea at Mr Lunn's, for in that case he would have lost sight of Jacob, who, in his impatience for the crop of lozenges, might scratch up the box again while he was absent, and carry it home – depriving him at once of reputation and guineas. No! he must think of nothing all the rest of this day, but of coaxing Jacob and keeping him out of mischief. It was a fatiguing and anxious evening to David; nevertheless, he dared not go to sleep without tying a piece of string to his thumb and great toe, to secure his frequent waking; for he meant to be up with the first peep of dawn, and be far out of reach before breakfast-time. His father, he thought, would certainly cut him off with a shilling; but what then? Such a striking young man as he would be sure to be well received in the West Indies: in foreign countries there are always openings – even for cats.[21] It was probable that some Princess Yarico would want him to marry her, and make him presents of very large jewels beforehand; after which, he needn't marry her unless he liked. David had made up his mind not to steal any more, even from people who were fond of him: it was an unpleasant way of making your fortune in a world where you were likely to be surprised in the act by brothers. Such alarms did not agree with David's constitution, and he had felt so much nausea this evening that no doubt his liver was affected. Besides, he would have been greatly hurt not to be thought well of in the world: he always meant to make a figure, and be thought worthy of the best seats and the best morsels.

Ruminating to this effect on the brilliant future in reserve for him, David by the help of his check-string kept himself on the alert to seize the time of earliest dawn for his rising and departure. His brothers, of course, were early risers, but he should anticipate them by at least an hour and a half, and the little room which he had to himself as only an occasional visitor, had its window over the horse-block, so that he could slip out through the window without the least difficulty. Jacob, the horrible Jacob, had an awkward trick of getting up before everybody else, to stem his hunger, by emptying the milk-bowl that was 'duly set'[22] for him; but of late he had taken to sleeping in the hay-loft, and if he came into the house, it would be on the opposite side to that from which David was making his exit. There was no need to think of Jacob; yet David was liberal enough to bestow a curse on him – it was the only thing he ever did bestow gratuitously. His small bundle of clothes was ready packed, and he was soon treading lightly on the steps of the horse-block, soon walking at a smart pace across the fields towards the thicket. It would take him no more than two minutes to get out the box; he could make out the tree it was under by the pale strip where the bark was off, although the dawning light was rather dimmer in the thicket. But what, in the name of – burnt pastry – was that large body with a staff planted beside it, close at the foot of the ash-tree? David paused, not to make up his mind as to the nature of the apparition – he had not the happiness of doubting for a moment that the staff was Jacob's pitchfork – but to gather the self-command necessary for addressing his brother with a sufficiently honeyed accent. Jacob was absorbed in scratching up the earth, and had not heard David's approach.

'I say, Jacob,' said David in a loud whisper, just as the tin box was lifted out of the hole.

Jacob looked up, and discerning his sweet-flavoured brother, nodded and grinned in the dim light in a way that made him seem to David like a triumphant demon. If he had been of an impetuous disposition, he would have snatched the pitchfork from the ground and impaled this fraternal demon. But David was by no means impetuous; he was a young man greatly given to calculate consequences, a habit which has been held to be the foundation of virtue.[23] But somehow it had not precisely that effect in David: he calculated whether an action would harm himself, or whether it would only harm other people. In the former case he was very timid about satisfying his immediate desires, but in the latter he would risk the result with much courage.

'Give it *me*, Jacob,' he said, stooping down and patting his brother. 'Let us see.'

Jacob, finding the lid rather tight, gave the box to his brother in perfect faith. David raised the lid, and shook his head, while Jacob put his finger in and took out a guinea to taste whether the metamorphosis into lozenges was complete and satisfactory.

'No, Jacob; too soon, too soon,' said David, when the guinea had been tasted. 'Give it me; we'll go and bury it somewhere else; we'll put it in yonder,' he added, pointing vaguely toward the distance.

David screwed on the lid, while Jacob, looking grave, rose and grasped his pitchfork. Then, seeing David's bundle, he snatched it, like a too officious Newfoundland, stuck his pitchfork into it and carried it over his shoulder in triumph as he accompanied David and the box out of the thicket.

What on earth was David to do? It would have been easy to frown at Jacob, and kick him, and order him to get away; but David dared as soon have kicked the bull. Jacob was quiet as long as he was treated indulgently; but on the slightest show of anger, he became unmanageable, and was liable to fits of fury which would have made him formidable even without his pitchfork. There was no mastery to be obtained over him except by kindness or guile. David tried guile.

'Go, Jacob,' he said, when they were out of the thicket – pointing towards the house as he spoke; 'go and fetch me a spade – a spade. But give *me* the bundle,' he added, trying to reach it from the fork, where it hung high above Jacob's tall shoulder.

But Jacob showed as much alacrity in obeying as a wasp shows in leaving a sugar-basin. Near David, he felt himself in the vicinity of lozenges: he chuckled and rubbed his brother's back, brandishing the bundle higher out of reach. David, with an inward groan, changed his tactics, and walked on as fast as he could. It was not safe to linger. Jacob would get tired of following him, or, at all events, could be eluded. If they could once get to the distant highroad, a coach would overtake them, David would mount it, having previously by some ingenious means secured his bundle, and then Jacob might howl and flourish his pitchfork as much as he liked. Meanwhile he was under the fatal necessity of being very kind to this ogre, and of providing a large breakfast for him when they stopped at a roadside inn. It was already three hours since they had started, and David was tired. Would no coach be coming up soon? he inquired. No coach for the next two hours. But there was a carrier's cart to come immediately, on its way to the next town. If he could slip out, even leaving his bundle behind, and get into the cart without Jacob! But there was a new obstacle. Jacob had recently discovered a remnant of sugar-candy in one of his brother's tail-pockets; and, since then, had cautiously kept his hold on that limb of the garment, perhaps with an expectation that there would be a further development of sugar-candy after a longer or shorter interval. Now every one who has worn a coat will understand the sensibilities that must keep a man from starting away in a hurry when there is a grasp on his coat-tail. David looked forward to being well received among strangers, but it might make a difference if he had only one tail to his coat.

He felt himself in a cold perspiration. He could walk no more: he must get into the cart and let Jacob get in with him. Presently a cheering idea occurred to him: after so large a breakfast, Jacob would be sure to go to sleep in the cart; you see at once that David meant to seize his bundle, jump out, and be free. His expectation was partly fulfilled: Jacob did go to sleep in the cart, but it was in a peculiar attitude – it was with his arms tightly fastened round his dear brother's body; and if ever David attempted to move, the grasp tightened with the force of an affectionate boa-constrictor.

'Th' innicent's fond on you,' observed the carrier, thinking that David was probably an amiable brother, and wishing to pay him a compliment.

David groaned. The ways of thieving were not ways of pleasantness.[24] Oh, why had he an idiot brother? Or why, in general, was the world so constituted that a man could not take his mother's guineas comfortably? David became grimly speculative.

Copious dinner at noon for Jacob; but little dinner, because little appetite, for David. Instead of eating, he plied Jacob with beer; for through this liberality he descried a hope. Jacob fell into a dead sleep, at last, *without* having his arms round David, who paid the reckoning, took his bundle, and walked off. In another half-hour he was on the coach on his way to Liverpool, smiling the smile of the triumphant wicked. He was rid of Jacob – he was bound for the Indies, where a gullible princess awaited him. He would never steal any more, but there would be no need; he would show himself so deserving, that people would make him presents freely. He must give up the notion of his father's legacy; but it was not likely he would ever want that trifle; and even if he did – why, it was a compensation to think that in being for ever divided from his family he was divided from Jacob, more terrible than Gorgon or Demogorgon[25] to David's timid green eyes. Thank heaven, he should never see Jacob any more!

CHAPTER 2

It was nearly six years after the departure of Mr David Faux for the West Indies, that the vacant shop in the market-place at Grimworth was understood to have been let to the stranger with a sallow complexion and a buff cravat, whose first appearance had caused some excitement in the bar of the Woolpack, where he had called to wait for the coach.

Grimworth, to a discerning eye, was a good place to set up shopkeeping in. There was no competition in it at present; the Church-people had their own grocer and draper; the Dissenters[1] had theirs; and the two or three butchers found a ready market for their joints without strict reference to religious persuasion – except that the rector's wife had given a general order for the veal sweet-breads and the mutton kidneys, while Mr Rodd, the Baptist minister, had requested that, so far as was compatible with the fair accommodation of other customers, the sheep's trotters might be reserved for him. And it was likely to be a growing place, for the trustees of Mr Zephaniah Crypt's Charity,[2] under the stimulus of a late visitation by commissioners, were beginning to apply long-accumulating funds to the rebuilding of the Yellow Coat School,[3] which was henceforth to be carried forward on a greatly-extended scale, the testator having left no restrictions concerning the curriculum, but only concerning the coat.

The shopkeepers at Grimworth were by no means unanimous as to the advantages promised by this prospect of increased population and trading, being substantial men, who liked doing a quiet business in which they were sure of their customers, and could calculate their returns to a nicety. Hitherto, it had been held a point of honour by the families in Grimworth parish, to buy their sugar and their flannel at the shops where their fathers and mothers had bought before them; but, if new-comers were to bring in the system of neck-and-neck trading, and solicit feminine eyes by gown-pieces laid in fan-like folds, and surmounted by artificial flowers, giving them a factitious charm

57

(for on what human figure would a gown sit like a fan, or what female head was like a bunch of China-asters?),[4] or, if new grocers were to fill their windows with mountains of currants and sugar, made seductive by contrast and tickets, – what security was there for Grimworth, that a vagrant spirit in shopping, once introduced, would not in the end carry the most important families to the larger market town of Cattle-ton, where, business being done on a system of small profits and quick returns, the fashions were of the freshest, and goods of all kinds might be bought at an advantage?

With this view of the times predominant among the tradespeople at Grimworth, their uncertainty concerning the nature of the business which the sallow-complexioned stranger was about to set up in the vacant shop, naturally gave some additional strength to the fears of the less sanguine. If he was going to sell drapery, it was probable that a pale-faced fellow like that would deal in showy and inferior articles – printed cottons and muslins which would leave their dye in the wash-tub, jobbed linen[5] full of knots, and flannel that would soon look like gauze. If grocery, then it was to be hoped that no mother of a family would trust the teas of an untried grocer. Such things had been known in some parishes as tradesmen going about canvassing for custom with cards in their pockets: when people came from nobody knew where, there was no knowing what they might do. It was a thousand pities that Mr Moffat, the auctioneer and broker, had died without leaving anybody to follow him in the business, and Mrs Cleve's trustee ought to have known better than to let a shop to a stranger. Even the discovery that ovens were being put up on the premises, and that the shop was, in fact, being fitted up for a confectioner and pastry-cook's business, hitherto unknown in Grimworth, did not quite suffice to turn the scale in the new-comer's favour, though the landlady at the Woolpack defended him warmly, said he seemed to be a very clever young man, and from what she could make out, came of a very good family; indeed, was most likely a good many people's betters.

It certainly made a blaze of light and colour, almost as if a rainbow had suddenly descended into the market-place, when, one fine morn-ing, the shutters were taken down[6] from the new shop, and the two windows displayed their decorations. On one side, there were the variegated tints of collared and marbled meats,[7] set off by bright green leaves, the pale brown of glazed pies, the rich tones of sauces and bottled fruits enclosed in their veil of glass – altogether a sight to bring tears into the eyes of a Dutch painter;[8] and on the other, there was a predominance of the more delicate hues of pink, and white, and yellow, and buff, in the abundant lozenges, candies, sweet biscuits and icings, which to the eyes of a bilious person might easily have been blended into a faëry landscape in Turner's latest style.[9] What a sight to dawn upon the eyes of Grimworth children! They almost forgot to go to their dinner that day, their appetites being preoccupied with imaginary sugar-plums; and I think even Punch, setting up his tabernacle[10] in the market-place, would not have succeeded in drawing them away from those shop-windows, where they stood according to gradations of size and strength, the biggest and strongest being nearest the window, and the little ones in the outermost rows lifting wide-open eyes and mouths towards the upper tier of jars, like small birds at meal-time.

The elder inhabitants pished and pshawed a little at the folly of the new shopkeeper in venturing on such an outlay in goods that would not keep; to be sure, Christmas was coming, but what housewife in Grimworth would not think shame to furnish forth her table with articles that were not home-cooked? No, no. Mr Edward Freely, as he called himself, was deceived, if he thought Grimworth money was to flow into his pockets on such terms.

Edward Freely was the name that shone in gilt letters on a mazarine[11] ground over the doorplace of the new shop – a generous-sounding name, that might have belonged to the open-hearted, improvident hero of an old comedy, who would have delighted in raining sugared almonds, like a new manna-gift,[12] among that small generation outside the windows. But Mr Edward Freely was a man whose impulses were kept in due subordination: he held that the desire for sweets and pastry must only be satisfied in a direct ratio with the power of paying for them. If the smallest child in Grimworth would go to him with a halfpenny in its tiny fist, he would, after ringing the halfpenny, deliver a just equivalent in 'rock.' He was not a man to cheat even the smallest child – he often said so, observing at the same time that he loved honesty, and also that he was very tender-hearted, though he didn't show his feelings as some people did.

Either in reward of such virtue, or according to some more hidden law of sequence, Mr Freely's business, in spite of prejudice, started under favourable auspices. For Mrs Chaloner, the rector's wife, was among the earliest customers at the shop, thinking it only right to encourage a new parishioner who had made a decorous appearance at church; and she found Mr Freely a most civil, obliging young man, and intelligent to a surprising degree for a confectioner; well-principled, too, for in giving her useful hints about choosing sugars he had thrown much light on the dishonesty of other tradesmen. Moreover, he had been in the West Indies, and had seen the very estate which had been her poor grandfather's property; and he said the missionaries were the only cause of the negro's discontent[13] – an observing young man, evidently. Mrs Chaloner ordered wine-biscuits and olives, and gave Mr Freely to understand that she should find his shop a great convenience. So did the doctor's wife, and so did Mrs Gate, at the large carding-mill,[14] who, having high connections frequently visiting her, might be expected to have a large consumption of ratafias[15] and macaroons.

The less aristocratic matrons of Grimworth seemed likely at first to justify their husbands' confidence that they would never pay a percentage of profits on drop-cakes, instead of making their own, or get up a hollow show of liberal housekeeping by purchasing slices of collared meat when a neighbour came in for supper. But it is my task to narrate the gradual corruption of Grimworth manners from their primitive simplicity – a melancholy task, if it were not cheered by the prospect of the fine peripateia[16] or downfall by which the progress of the corruption was ultimately checked.

It was young Mrs Steene, the veterinary surgeon's wife, who first gave way to temptation. I fear she had been rather over-educated for her station in life, for she knew by heart many passages in 'Lalla Rookh,' the 'Corsair,' and the 'Siege of Corinth,'[17] which had given her a distaste for domestic occupations, and caused her a withering disappointment at the discovery that Mr Steene, since his marriage, had lost all interest in the 'bulbul,'[18] openly preferred discussing the nature of spavin[19] with a coarse neighbour, and was angry if the pudding turned out watery – indeed, was simply a top-booted[20] 'vet.,' who came in hungry at dinner-time; and not in the least like a nobleman turned Corsair out of pure scorn for his race, or like a renegade[21] with a turban and crescent, unless it were in the irritability of his temper. And scorn is such a very different thing in top-boots!

This brutal man had invited a supper-party for Christmas eve, when he would expect to see mince-pies on the table. Mrs Steene had prepared her mince-meat, and had devoted much butter, fine flour, and labour, to the making of a batch of pies in the morning; but they proved to be so very heavy when they came out of the oven, that she could only think with trembling of the moment when her husband should catch sight of them on the supper-table. He would storm at her, she was certain; and before all the company; and then she should never help crying: it was so dreadful to think she had come to that, after the bulbul and everything! Suddenly the thought darted through her mind that *this once* she might send for a dish of mince-pies from Freely's: she knew he had some. But what was to become of the eighteen heavy mince-pies? Oh, it was of no use thinking about that; it was very expensive – indeed, making mince-pies at all was a great expense, when they were not sure to turn out well: it would be much better to buy them ready-made. You paid a little more for them, but there was no risk of waste.

Such was the sophistry with which this misguided young woman – enough. Mrs Steene sent for the mince-pies, and, I am grieved to add, garbled[22] her household accounts in order to conceal the fact from her husband. This was the second step in a downward course, all owing to a young woman's being out of harmony with her circumstances, yearning after renegades and bulbuls, and being subject to claims from a veterinary surgeon fond of mince-pies. The third step was to harden herself by telling the fact of the bought mince-pies to her intimate friend Mrs Mole, who had already guessed it, and who subsequently encouraged herself in buying a mould of jelly, instead of exerting her own skill, by the reflection that 'other people' did the same sort of thing. The infection spread; soon there was a party or clique in Grimworth on the side of 'buying at Freely's;' and many husbands, kept for some time in the dark on this point, innocently swallowed at two mouthfuls a tart on which they were paying a profit of a hundred per cent, and as innocently encouraged a fatal disingenuousness in the partners of their bosoms by praising the pastry. Others, more keen-sighted, winked at the too frequent presentation on washing-days, and at impromptu suppers, of superior spiced-beef, which flattered their palates more than the cold remnants they had formerly been contented with. Every housewife who had once 'bought at Freely's' felt a secret joy when she detected a similar perversion in her neighbour's practice, and soon only two or three old-fashioned mistresses of families held out in the protest against the growing demoralisation, saying to their neighbours who came to sup with them, 'I can't offer you Freely's beef, or Freely's cheese-cakes; everything in our house is home-made; I'm afraid you'll hardly have any appetite for our plain pastry.' The doctor, whose cook was not satisfactory, the curate, who kept no cook, and the mining agent, who was a great *bon vivant*, even began to rely on Freely for the greater part of their dinner, when they wished to give an entertainment of some brilliancy. In short, the business of manufacturing the more fanciful viands was fast passing out of the hands of maids and matrons in private families, and was becoming the work of a special commercial organ.

I am not ignorant that this sort of thing is called the inevitable course of civilisation, division of labour,[23] and so forth, and that the maids and matrons may be said to have had their hands set free from cookery to add to the wealth of society in some other way. Only it happened at Grimworth, which, to be sure, was a low place, that the maids and matrons could do nothing with their hands at all better than cooking; not even those who had always made heavy cakes and leathery pastry. And so it came to pass, that the progress of civilisation at Grimworth was not otherwise apparent than in the impoverishment of men, the gossiping idleness of women, and the heightening prosperity of Mr Edward Freely.

The Yellow Coat School was a double source of profit to the calculating confectioner; for he opened an eating-room for the superior workmen employed on the new school, and he accommodated the pupils at the old school by giving great attention to the fancy-sugar department. When I think of the sweet-tasted swans and other ingenious white shapes crunched by the small teeth of that rising generation, I am glad to remember that a certain amount of calcareous[24] food has been held good for young creatures whose bones are not quite formed; for I have observed these delicacies to have an inorganic flavour which would have recommended them greatly to that young lady of the 'Spectator's' acquaintance[25] who habitually made her dessert on the stems of tobacco-pipes.

As for the confectioner himself, he made his way gradually into Grimworth homes, as his commodities did, in spite of some initial repugnance. Somehow or other, his reception as a guest seemed a thing that required justifying, like the purchasing of his pastry. In the first place, he was a stranger, and therefore open to suspicion; secondly, the confectionery business was so entirely new at Grimworth, that its place in the scale of rank had not been distinctly ascertained. There was no doubt about drapers and grocers, when they came of good old Grimworth families, like Mr Luff and Mr Prettyman: they visited with the Palfreys, who farmed their own land, played many a game at whist with the doctor, and condescended a little towards the timber-merchant, who had lately taken to the coal-trade also, and had got new furniture; but whether a confectioner should be admitted to this higher level of respectability, or should be understood to find his associates among butchers and bakers, was a new question on which tradition threw no light. His being a bachelor was in his favour, and would perhaps have been enough to turn the scale, even if Mr Edward Freely's other personal pretensions had been of an entirely insignificant cast. But so far from this, it very soon appeared that he was a remarkable young man, who had been in the West Indies, and had seen many wonders by sea and land, so that he could charm the ears of Grimworth Desdemonas[26] with stories of strange fishes, especially sharks, which he had stabbed in the nick of time by bravely plunging overboard just as the monster was turning on his side to devour the cook's mate; of terrible fevers which he had undergone in a land where the wind blows from all quarters at once; of rounds of toast cut straight from the bread-fruit trees; of toes bitten off by land-crabs; of large honours that had been offered to him as a man who knew what was what, and was therefore particularly needed in a tropical climate; and of a Creole heiress[27] who had wept bitterly at his departure. Such conversational talents as these, we know, will overcome disadvantages of complexion; and young Towers, whose cheeks were of the finest pink, set off by a fringe of dark whisker, was quite eclipsed by the presence of the sallow Mr Freely. So exceptional a confectioner elevated his business, and might well begin to make disengaged hearts flutter a little.

Fathers and mothers were naturally more slow and cautious in their recognition of the new-comer's merits.

'He's an amusing fellow,' said Mr Prettyman, the highly respectable grocer. (Mrs Prettyman was a Miss Fothergill, and her sister had married a London mercer.)[28] 'He's an amusing fellow; and I've no objection to his making one at the Oyster Club; but he's a bit too fond of riding the high horse. He's uncommonly knowing, I'll allow; but how came he to go to the Indies? I should like that answered. It's unnatural in a confectioner. I'm not fond of people that have been beyond seas, if they can't give a good account how they happened to go. When folks go so far off, it's because they've got little credit nearer home – that's my opinion. However, he's got some good rum; but I don't want to be hand and glove with him, for all that.'

It was this kind of dim suspicion which beclouded the view of Mr Freely's qualities in the maturer minds of Grimworth through the early months of his residence there. But when the confectioner ceased to be a novelty, the suspicions also ceased to be novel, and people got tired of hinting at them, especially as they seemed to be refuted by his advancing prosperity and importance. Mr Freely was becoming a person of influence in the parish; he was found useful as an overseer of the poor,[29] having great firmness in enduring other people's pain, which firmness, he said, was due to his great benevolence; he always did what was good for people in the end. Mr Chaloner had even selected him as clergyman's church-warden, for he was a very handy man, and much more of Mr Chaloner's opinion in everything about church business than the older parishioners. Mr Freely was a very regular churchman, but at the Oyster Club he was sometimes a little free in his conversation, more than hinting at a life of Sultanic self-indulgence which he had passed in the West Indies, shaking his head now and then and smiling rather bitterly, as men are wont to do when they intimate that they have become a little too wise to be instructed about a world which has long been flat and stale[30] to them.

For some time he was quite general in his attentions to the fair sex, combining the gallantries of a lady's man with a severity of criticism on the person and manners of absent belles, which tended rather to stimulate in the feminine breast the desire to conquer the approval of so fastidious a judge. Nothing short of the very best in the department of female charms and virtues could suffice to kindle the ardour of Mr Edward Freely, who had become familiar with the most luxuriant and dazzling beauty in the West Indies. It may seem incredible that a confectioner should have ideas and conversation so much resembling those to be met with in a higher walk of life, but it must be remembered that he had not merely travelled, he had also bow-legs and a sallow, small-featured visage, so that nature herself had stamped him for a fastidious connoisseur of the fair sex.

At last, however, it seemed clear that Cupid had found a sharper arrow than usual, and that Mr Freely's heart was pierced. It was the general talk among the young people at Grimworth. But was it really love? and not rather ambition? Miss Fullilove, the timber-merchant's daughter, was quite sure that if *she* were Miss Penny Palfrey, she would be cautious; it was not a good sign when men looked so much above themselves for a wife. For it was no less a person than Miss Penelope Palfrey, second daughter of the Mr Palfrey who farmed his own land, that had attracted Mr Freely's peculiar regard, and conquered his fastidiousness; and no wonder; for the Ideal, as exhibited in the finest waxwork, was perhaps never so closely approached by the Real[31] as in the person of the pretty Penelope. Her yellowish flaxen hair did not curl naturally, I admit, but its bright crisp ringlets were such smooth, perfect miniature tubes, that you would have longed to pass your little finger through them, and feel their soft elasticity. She wore them in a crop,[32] for in those days, when society was in a healthier state, young ladies wore crops long after they were twenty, and Penelope was not yet nineteen. Like the waxen ideal, she had round blue eyes, and round nostrils in her little nose, and teeth such as the ideal would be seen to have, if it ever showed them. Altogether, she was a small, round thing, as neat as a pink and white double daisy, and as guileless; for I hope it does not argue guile in a pretty damsel of nineteen, to think that she should like to have a beau and be 'engaged,' when her elder sister had already been in that position a year and a half. To be sure, there was young Towers always coming to the house; but Penny felt convinced he only came to see her brother, for he never had anything to say to her, and never offered her his arm, and was as awkward and silent as possible.

It is not unlikely that Mr Freely had early been smitten by Penny's charms, as brought under his observation at church, but he had to make his way in society a little before he could come into nearer contact with them; and even after he was well received in Grimworth families, it was a long while before he could converse with Penny otherwise than in an incidental meeting at Mr Luff's. It was not so easy to get invited to Long Meadows, the residence of the Palfreys; for though Mr Palfrey had been losing money of late years, not being able quite to recover his feet after the terrible murrain[33] which forced him to borrow, his family were far from considering themselves on the same level even as the old-established tradespeople with whom they visited.

The greatest people, even kings and queens, must visit with somebody, and the equals of the great are scarce. They were especially scarce at Grimworth, which, as I have before observed, was a low parish, mentioned with the most scornful brevity in gazetteers.[34] Even the great people there were far behind those of their own standing in other parts of this realm. Mr Palfrey's farmyard doors had the paint all worn off them, and the front garden walks had long been merged in a general weediness. Still, his father had been called Squire Palfrey, and had been respected by the last Grimworth generation as a man who could afford to drink too much in his own house.

Pretty Penny was not blind to the fact that Mr Freely admired her, and she felt sure that it was he who had sent her a beautiful valentine; but her sister seemed to think so lightly of him (all young ladies think lightly of the gentlemen to whom they are not engaged), that Penny never dared mention him, and trembled and blushed whenever they met him, thinking of the valentine, which was very strong in its expressions, and which she felt guilty of knowing by heart. A man who had been to the Indies, and knew the sea so well, seemed to her a sort of public character, almost like Robinson Crusoe or Captain Cook;[35] and Penny had always wished her husband to be a remarkable personage, likely to be put in Mangnall's Questions,[36] with which register of the immortals she had become acquainted during her one year at a boarding-school. Only it seemed strange that a remarkable man should be a confectioner and pastry-cook, and this anomaly quite disturbed Penny's dreams. Her brothers, she knew, laughed at men who couldn't sit on horseback well, and called them tailors; but her brothers were very rough, and were quite without that power of anecdote which made Mr Freely such a delightful companion. He was a very good man, she thought, for she had heard him say at Mr Luff's, one day, that he always wished to do his duty in whatever state of life he might be placed; and he knew a great deal of poetry, for one day he had repeated a verse of a song. She wondered if he had made the words of the valentine! – it ended in this way: –

> 'Without thee, it is pain to live,
> But with thee, it were sweet to die.'[37]

Poor Mr Freely! her father would very likely object – she felt sure he would, for he always called Mr Freely 'that sugar-plum fellow.' Oh, it was very cruel, when true love was crossed in that way, and all because Mr Freely was a confectioner: well, Penny would be true to him, for all that, and since his being a confectioner gave her an opportunity of showing her faithfulness, she was glad of it. Edward Freely was a pretty name, much better than John Towers. Young Towers had offered her a rose out of his button-hole the other day, blushing very much; but she refused it, and thought with delight how much Mr Freely would be comforted if he knew her firmness of mind.

Poor little Penny! the days were so very long among the daisies on a grazing farm, and thought is so active – how was it possible that the inward drama should not get the start of the outward? I have known young ladies, much better educated, and with an outward world diversified by instructive lectures, to say nothing of literature and highly-developed fancy-work, who have spun a cocoon of visionary joys and sorrows for themselves, just as Penny did. Her elder sister Letitia, who had a prouder style of beauty, and a more worldly ambition, was engaged to a wool-factor,[38] who came all the way from Cattelton to see her; and everybody knows that a wool-factor takes a very high rank, sometimes driving a double-bodied gig.[39] Letty's notions got higher every day, and Penny never dared to speak of her cherished griefs to her lofty sister – never dared to propose that they should call at Mr Freely's to buy liquorice,[40] though she had prepared for such an incident by mentioning a slight sore throat. So she had to pass the shop on the other side of the market-place, and reflect, with a suppressed sigh, that behind those pink and white jars somebody was thinking of her tenderly, unconscious of the small space that divided her from him.

And it was quite true that, when business permitted, Mr Freely thought a great deal of Penny. He thought her prettiness comparable to the loveliest things in confectionery; he judged her to be of submissive temper – likely to wait upon him as well as if she had been a negress, and to be silently terrified when his liver made him irritable; and he considered the Palfrey family quite the best in the parish, possessing marriageable daughters. On the whole, he thought her worthy to become Mrs Edward Freely, and all the more so, because it would probably require some ingenuity to win her. Mr Palfrey was capable of horse-whipping a too rash pretender to his daughter's hand; and, moreover, he had three tall sons: it was clear that a suitor would be at a disadvantage with such a family, unless travel and natural acumen had given him a countervailing power of contrivance. And the first idea that occurred to him in the matter was, that Mr Palfrey would object less if he knew that the Freelys were a much higher family than his own. It had been foolish modesty in him hitherto to conceal the fact that a branch of the Freelys held a manor in Yorkshire, and to shut up the portrait of his great uncle the admiral, instead of hanging it up where a family portrait should be hung – over the mantelpiece in the parlour. Admiral Freely, K.C.B.,[41] once placed in this conspicuous position, was seen to have had one arm only, and one eye, – in these points resembling the heroic Nelson,[42] – while a certain pallid insignificance of feature confirmed the relationship between himself and his grand-nephew.

Next, Mr Freely was seized with an irrepressible ambition to possess Mrs Palfrey's receipt for brawn, hers being pronounced on all hands to be superior to his own – as he informed her in a very flattering letter carried by his errand-boy. Now Mrs Palfrey, like other geniuses, wrought by instinct rather than by rule, and possessed no receipts, – indeed, despised all people who used them, observing that people who pickled by book, must pickle by weights and measures, and such nonsense; as for herself, her weights and measures were the tip of her finger and the tip of her tongue, and if you went nearer, why, of course, for dry goods like flour and spice, you went by handfuls and pinches, and for wet, there was a middle-sized jug – quite the best thing whether for much or little, because you might know how much a teacupful was if you'd got any use of your senses, and you might be sure it would take five middle-sized jugs to make a gallon. Knowledge of this kind is like Titian's colouring[43] difficult to communicate; and as Mrs Palfrey, once remarkably handsome, had now become rather stout and asthmatical, and scarcely ever left home, her oral teaching could hardly be given anywhere except at Long Meadows. Even a matron is not insusceptible to flattery, and the prospect of a visitor whose great object would be to listen to her conversation, was not without its charms to Mrs Palfrey. Since there was no receipt to be sent in reply to Mr Freely's humble request, she called on her more docile daughter, Penny, to write a note, telling him that her mother would be glad to see him and talk with him on brawn, any day that he could call at Long Meadows. Penny obeyed with a trembling hand, thinking how wonderfully things came about in this world.

CHAPTER 2

In this way, Mr Freely got himself introduced into the home of the Palfreys, and notwithstanding a tendency in the male part of the family to jeer at him a little as 'peaky' and bow-legged, he presently established his position as an accepted and frequent guest. Young Towers looked at him with increasing disgust when they met at the house on a Sunday, and secretly longed to try his ferret upon him, as a piece of vermin which that valuable animal would be likely to tackle with unhesitating vigour. But – so blind sometimes are parents – neither Mr nor Mrs Palfrey suspected that Penny would have anything to say to a trades-man of questionable rank whose youthful bloom was much withered. Young Towers, they thought, had an eye to her, and *that* was likely enough to be a match some day; but Penny was a child at present. And all the while Penny was imagining the circumstances under which Mr Freely would make her an offer: perhaps down by the row of damson-trees, when they were in the garden before tea; perhaps by letter – in which case, how would the letter begin? 'Dearest Penelope?' or 'My dear Miss Penelope?' or straight off, without dear anything, as seemed the most natural when people were embarrassed? But, however he might make the offer, she would not accept it without her father's consent: she would always be true to Mr Freely, but she would not disobey her father. For Penny was a good girl, though some of her female friends were afterwards of opinion that it spoke ill for her not to have felt an instinctive repugnance to Mr Freely.

But he was cautious, and wished to be quite sure of the ground he trod on. His views in marriage were not entirely sentimental, but were as duly mingled with considerations of what would be advantageous to a man in his position, as if he had had a very large amount of money spent on his education. He was not a man to fall in love in the wrong place; and so, he applied himself quite as much to conciliate the favour of the parents, as to secure the attachment of Penny. Mrs Palfrey had not been inaccessible to flattery, and her husband, being also of mortal mould, would not, it might be hoped, be proof against rum – that very fine Jamaica rum of which Mr Freely expected always to have a supply sent him from Jamaica. It was not easy to get Mr Palfrey into the parlour behind the shop, where a mild back-street light fell on the features of the heroic admiral; but by getting hold of him rather late one evening as he was about to return home from Grimworth, the aspiring lover succeeded in persuading him to sup on some collared beef which, after Mrs Palfrey's brawn, he would find the very best of cold eating.

From that hour Mr Freely felt sure of success: being in privacy with an estimable man old enough to be his father, and being rather lonely in the world, it was natural he should unbosom himself a little on subjects which he could not speak of in a mixed circle – especially concerning his expectations from his uncle in Jamaica, who had no children, and loved his nephew Edward better than any one else in the world, though he had been so hurt at his leaving Jamaica, that he had threatened to cut him off with a shilling. However, he had since written to state his full forgiveness, and though he was an eccentric old gentleman and could not bear to give away money during his life, Mr Edward Freely could show Mr Palfrey the letter which declared, plainly enough, who would be the affectionate uncle's heir. Mr Palfrey actually saw the letter, and could not help admiring the spirit of the nephew who declared that such brilliant hopes as these made no difference to his conduct; he should work at his humble business and make his modest fortune at it all the same. If the Jamaica estate was to come to him – well and good. It was nothing very surprising for one of the Freely family to have an estate left him, considering the lands that family had possessed in time gone by, – nay, still possessed in the Northumberland branch. Would not Mr Palfrey take another glass of rum? and also look at the last year's balance of the accounts? Mr Freely was a man who cared to possess personal virtues, and did not pique himself on his family, though some men would.

We know how easily the great Leviathan[44] may be led, when once there is a hook in his nose or a bridle in his jaws. Mr Palfrey was a large man, but, like Leviathan's, his bulk went against him when once he had taken a turning. He was not a mercurial man, who easily changed his point of view. Enough. Before two months were over, he had given his consent to Mr Freely's marriage with his daughter Penny, and having hit on a formula by which he could justify it, fenced off all doubts and objections, his own included. The formula was this: 'I'm not a man to put my head[45] up an entry before I know where it leads.'

Little Penny was very proud and fluttering, but hardly so happy as she expected to be in an engagement. She wondered if young Towers cared much about it, for he had not been to the house lately, and her sister and brothers were rather inclined to sneer than to sympathise.

Grimworth rang with the news. All men extolled Mr Freely's good fortune; while the women, with the tender solicitude characteristic of the sex, wished the marriage might turn out well.

While affairs were at this triumphant juncture, Mr Freely one morning observed that a stone-carver who had been breakfasting in the eating-room had left a newspaper behind. It was the 'X—shire Gazette,' and X—shire being a county not unknown to Mr Freely, he felt some curiosity to glance over it, and especially over the advertisements. A slight flush came over his face as he read. It was produced by the following announcement: – 'If David Faux, son of Jonathan Faux, late of Gilsbrook, will apply at the office of Mr Strutt, attorney, of Rodham, he will hear of something to his advantage.'

'Father's dead!' exclaimed Mr Freely, involuntarily. 'Can he have left me a legacy?'

CHAPTER 3

Perhaps it was a result quite different from your expectations, that Mr David Faux should have returned from the West Indies only a few years after his arrival there, and have set up in his old business, like any plain man who had never travelled. But these cases do occur in life. Since, as we know, men change their skies and see new constellations without changing their souls, it will follow sometimes that they don't change their business under those novel circumstances.

Certainly, this result was contrary to David's own expectations. He had looked forward, you are aware, to a brilliant career among 'the blacks;' but, either because they had already seen too many white men, or for some other reason, they did not at once recognise him as a superior order of human being; besides, there were no princesses among them. Nobody in Jamaica was anxious to maintain David for the mere pleasure of his society; and those hidden merits of a man which are so well known to himself were as little recognised there as they notoriously are in the effete society of the Old World. So that in the dark hints that David threw out at the Oyster Club about that life of Sultanic self-indulgence spent by him in the luxurious Indies, I really think he was doing himself a wrong; I believe he worked for his bread, and, in fact, took to cooking again, as, after all, the only department in which he could offer skilled labour. He had formed several ingenious plans by which he meant to circumvent people of large fortune and small faculty; but then he never met with exactly the right people under exactly the right circumstances. David's devices for getting rich without work had apparently no direct relation with the world outside him, as his confectionery receipts had. It is possible to pass a great many bad halfpennies and bad half-crowns, but I believe there has no instance been known of passing a halfpenny or a half-crown as a sovereign. A sharper[1] can drive a brisk trade in this world: it is undeniable that there may be a fine career for him, if he will dare consequences; but David was too timid to be a sharper, or venture in

72

any way among the man-traps of the law. He dared rob nobody but his mother. And so he had to fall back on the genuine value there was in him – to be content to pass as a good halfpenny, or, to speak more accurately, as a good confectioner. For in spite of some additional reading and observation, there was nothing else he could make so much money by; nay, he found in himself even a capability of extending his skill in this direction, and embracing all forms of cookery; while, in other branches of human labour, he began to see that it was not possible for him to shine. Fate was too strong for him; he had thought to master her inclination and had fled over the seas to that end; but she caught him, tied an apron round him, and snatching him from all other devices, made him devise cakes and patties in a kitchen at Kingstown. He was getting submissive to her, since she paid him with tolerable gains; but fevers and prickly heat, and other evils incidental to cooks in ardent climates, made him long for his native land; so he took ship once more, carrying his six years' savings, and seeing distinctly, this time, what were Fate's² intentions as to his career. If you question me closely as to whether all the money with which he set up at Grimworth consisted of pure and simple earnings, I am obliged to confess that he got a sum or two for charitably abstaining from mentioning some other people's misdemeanours. Altogether, since no prospects were attached to his family name, and since a new christening seemed a suitable commencement of a new life, Mr David Faux thought it as well to call himself Mr Edward Freely.

But lo! now, in opposition to all calculable probability, some benefit appeared to be attached to his name of David Faux. Should he neglect it, as beneath the attention of a prosperous tradesman? It might bring him into contact with his family again, and he felt no yearnings in that direction: moreover, he had small belief that the 'something to his advantage' could be anything considerable. On the other hand, even a small gain is pleasant, and the promise of it in this instance was so surprising, that David felt his curiosity awakened. The scale dipped at last on the side of writing to the lawyer, and, to be brief, the correspond-ence ended in an appointment for a meeting between David and his eldest brother at Mr Strutt's, the vague 'something' having been defined as a legacy from his father of eighty-two pounds three shillings.

David, you know, had expected to be disinherited; and so he would have been, if he had not, like some other indifferent sons, come of excellent parents, whose conscience made them scrupulous where much more highly-instructed people often feel themselves warranted in following the bent of their indignation. Good Mrs Faux could never forget that she had brought this ill-conditioned son into the world when he was in that entirely helpless state which excluded the smallest choice on his part; and, somehow or other, she felt that his going wrong would be his father's and mother's fault, if they failed in one tittle of their parental duty. Her notion of parental duty was not of a high and subtle kind, but it included giving him his due share of the family property; for when a man had got a little honest money of his own, was he so likely to steal? To cut the delinquent son off with a shilling, was like delivering him over to his evil propensities. No; let the sum of twenty guineas which he had stolen be deducted from his share, and then let the sum of three guineas be put back from it, seeing that his mother had always considered three of the twenty guineas as his; and, though he had run away, and was, perhaps, gone across the sea, let the money be left to him all the same, and be kept in reserve for his possible return. Mr Faux agreed to his wife's views, and made a codicil to his will accordingly, in time to die with a clear conscience. But for some time his family thought it likely that David would never reappear; and the eldest son, who had the charge of Jacob on his hands, often thought it a little hard that David might perhaps be dead, and yet, for want of certitude on that point, his legacy could not fall to his legal heir. But in this state of things the opposite certitude – namely, that David was still alive and in England – seemed to be brought by the testimony of a neighbour, who, having been on a journey to Cattelton, was pretty sure he had seen David in a gig, with a stout man driving by his side. He could 'swear it was David,' though he could 'give no account why, for he had no marks on him; but no more had a white dog, and that didn't hinder folks from knowing a white dog.' It was this incident which had led to the advertisement.

The legacy was paid, of course, after a few preliminary disclosures as to Mr David's actual position. He begged to send his love to his mother, and to say that he hoped to pay her a dutiful visit by-and-by; but, at present, his business and near prospect of marriage made it difficult for him to leave home. His brother replied with much frankness.

'My mother may do as she likes about having you to see her, but,

for my part, I don't want to catch sight of you on the premises again.
When folks have taken a new name, they'd better keep to their new
'quinetance.'

David pocketed the insult along with the eighty-two pounds three,
and travelled home again in some triumph at the ease of a transaction
which had enriched him to this extent. He had no intention of offending
his brother by further claims on his fraternal recognition, and relapsed
with full contentment into the character of Mr Edward Freely, the
orphan, scion of a great but reduced family, with an eccentric uncle in
the West Indies. (I have already hinted that he had some acquaintance
with imaginative literature; and being of a practical turn, he had, you
perceive, applied even this form of knowledge to practical purposes.)

It was little more than a week after the return from his fruitful
journey, that the day of his marriage with Penny having been fixed, it
was agreed that Mrs Palfrey should overcome her reluctance to move
from home, and that she and her husband should bring their two
daughters to inspect little Penny's future abode and decide on the new
arrangements to be made for the reception of the bride. Mr Freely
meant her to have a house so pretty and comfortable that she need not
envy even a wool-factor's wife. Of course, the upper room over the
shop was to be the best sitting-room; but also the parlour behind the
shop was to be made a suitable bower for the lovely Penny, who would
naturally wish to be near her husband, though Mr Freely declared his
resolution never to allow *his* wife to wait in the shop. The decisions
about the parlour furniture were left till last, because the party was to
take tea there; and, about five o'clock, they were all seated there with
the best muffins and buttered buns before them, little Penny blushing
and smiling, with her 'crop' in the best order, and a blue frock showing
her little white shoulders, while her opinion was being always asked
and never given. She secretly wished to have a particular sort of
chimney ornaments, but she could not have brought herself to mention
it. Seated by the side of her yellow and rather withered lover, who,
though he had not reached his thirtieth year, had already crow's-feet
about his eyes, she was quite tremulous at the greatness of her lot in
being married to a man who had travelled so much – and before her
sister Letty! The handsome Letitia looked rather proud and contemptuous, thought her future brother-in-law an odious person, and
was vexed with her father and mother for letting Penny marry him.

Dear little Penny! She certainly did look like a fresh white-heart cherry going to be bitten off the stem by that lipless mouth. Would no deliverer come to make a slip between that cherry and that mouth without a lip?[3]

'Quite a family likeness between the admiral and you, Mr Freely,' observed Mrs Palfrey, who was looking at the family portrait for the first time. 'It's wonderful! and only a grand-uncle. Do you feature the rest of your family, as you know of?'

'I can't say,' said Mr Freely, with a sigh. 'My family have mostly thought themselves too high to take any notice of me.'

At this moment an extraordinary disturbance was heard in the shop, as of a heavy animal stamping about and making angry noises, and then of a glass vessel falling in shivers, while the voice of the apprentice was heard calling 'Master' in great alarm.

Mr Freely rose in anxious astonishment, and hastened into the shop, followed by the four Palfreys, who made a group at the parlour-door, transfixed with wonder at seeing a large man in a smock-frock, with a pitchfork in his hand, rush up to Mr Freely and hug him, crying out, – 'Zavy, Zavy, b'other Zavy!'

It was Jacob, and for some moments David lost all presence of mind. He felt arrested for having stolen his mother's guineas. He turned cold, and trembled in his brother's grasp.

'Why, how's this?' said Mr Palfrey, advancing from the door. 'Who is he?'

Jacob supplied the answer by saying over and over again, –

'I'se Zacob, b'other Zacob. Come 'o zee Zavy' – till hunger prompted him to relax his grasp, and to seize a large raised pie, which he lifted to his mouth.

By this time David's power of device had begun to return, but it was a very hard task for his prudence to master his rage and hatred towards poor Jacob.

'I don't know who he is; he must be drunk,' he said, in a low tone to Mr Palfrey. 'But he's dangerous with that pitchfork. He'll never let it go.' Then checking himself on the point of betraying too great an intimacy with Jacob's habits, he added, '*You* watch him, while I run for the constable.' And he hurried out of the shop.

'Why, where do you come from, my man?' said Mr Palfrey, speaking to Jacob in a conciliatory tone. Jacob was eating his pie by large mouthfuls, and looking round at the other good things in the shop, while he embraced his pitchfork with his left arm and laid his left hand on some Bath buns. He was in the rare position of a person who recovers a long absent friend and finds him richer than ever in the characteristics that won his heart.

'I's Zacob – b'other Zacob – 't home. I love Zavy – b'other Zavy,' he said, as soon as Mr Palfrey had drawn his attention. 'Zavy come back from z' Indies – got mother's zinnies. Where's Zavy?' he added, looking round and then turning to the others with a questioning air, puzzled by David's disappearance.

'It's very odd,' observed Mr Palfrey to his wife and daughters. 'He seems to say Freely's his brother come back from th' Indies.'

'What a pleasant relation for us!' said Letitia, sarcastically. 'I think he's a good deal like Mr Freely. He's got just the same sort of nose, and his eyes are the same colour.'

Poor Penny was ready to cry.

But now Mr Freely re-entered the shop without the constable. During his walk of a few yards he had had time and calmness enough to widen his view of consequences, and he saw that to get Jacob taken to the workhouse or to the lock-up house as an offensive stranger, might have awkward effects if his family took the trouble of inquiring after him. He must resign himself to more patient measures.

'On second thoughts,' he said, beckoning to Mr Palfrey and whispering to him while Jacob's back was turned, 'he's a poor half-witted fellow. Perhaps his friends will come after him. I don't mind giving him something to eat, and letting him lie down for the night. He's got it into his head that he knows me – they do get these fancies, idiots do. He'll perhaps go away again in an hour or two, and make no more ado. I'm a kind-hearted man *myself* – I shouldn't like to have the poor fellow ill-used.'

'Why, he'll eat a sovereign's worth in no time,' said Mr Palfrey, thinking Mr Freely a little too magnificent in his generosity.

'Eh, Zavy, come back?' exclaimed Jacob, giving his dear brother another hug, which crushed Mr Freely's features inconveniently against the stale[4] of the pitchfork.

'Ay, ay,' said Mr Freely, smiling, with every capability of murder in his mind, except the courage to commit it. He wished the Bath buns might by chance have arsenic in them.

'Mother's zinnies?' said Jacob, pointing to a glass jar of yellow lozenges that stood in the window. 'Zive 'em me.'

David dared not do otherwise than reach down the glass jar and give Jacob a handful. He received them in his smock-frock, which he held out for more.

'They'll keep him quiet a bit, at any rate,' thought David, and emptied the jar. Jacob grinned and mowed with delight.

'You're very good to this stranger, Mr Freely,' said Letitia; and then spitefully, as David joined the party at the parlour-door, 'I think you could hardly treat him better, if he was really your brother.'

'I've always thought it a duty to be good to idiots,' said Mr Freely, striving after the most moral view of the subject. 'We might have been idiots ourselves – everybody might have been born idiots, instead of having their right senses.'

'I don't know where there'd ha' been victual for us all then,' observed Mrs Palfrey, regarding the matter in a housewifely light.

'But let us sit down again and finish our tea,' said Mr Freely. 'Let us leave the poor creature to himself.'

They walked into the parlour again; but Jacob, not apparently appreciating the kindness of leaving him to himself, immediately followed his brother, and seated himself, pitchfork grounded, at the table.

'Well,' said Miss Letitia, rising, 'I don't know whether *you* mean to stay, mother; but I shall go home.'

'Oh, me too,' said Penny, frightened to death at Jacob, who had begun to nod and grin at her.

'Well, I think we *had* better be going, Mr Palfrey,' said the mother, rising more slowly.

Mr Freely, whose complexion had become decidedly yellower during the last half-hour, did not resist this proposition. He hoped they should meet again 'under happier circumstances.'

'It's my belief the man is his brother,' said Letitia, when they were all on their way home.

'Letty, it's very ill-natured of you,' said Penny, beginning to cry.

'Nonsense!' said Mr Palfrey. 'Freely's got no brother – he's said so many and many a time; he's an orphan; he's got nothing but uncles – leastwise, one. What's it matter what an idiot says? What call had Freely to tell lies?'

Letitia tossed her head and was silent.

Mr Freely, left alone with his affectionate brother Jacob, brooded over the possibility of luring him out of the town early the next morning, and getting him conveyed to Gilsbrook without further betrayals. But the thing was difficult. He saw clearly that if he took Jacob away himself, his absence, conjoined with the disappearance of the stranger, would either cause the conviction that he was really a relative, or would oblige him to the dangerous course of inventing a story to account for his disappearance, and his own absence at the same time. David groaned. There come occasions when falsehood is felt to be inconvenient. It would, perhaps, have been a longer-headed device, if he had never told any of those clever fibs about his uncles, grand and otherwise; for the Palfreys were simple people, and shared the popular prejudice against lying. Even if he could get Jacob away this time, what security was there that he would not come again, having once found the way? O guineas! O lozenges! what enviable people those were who had never robbed their mothers, and had never told fibs! David spent a sleepless night, while Jacob was snoring close by. Was this the upshot of travelling to the Indies, and acquiring experience combined with anecdote?

He rose at break of day, as he had once before done when he was in fear of Jacob, and took all gentle means to rouse this fatal brother from his deep sleep; he dared not be loud, because his apprentice was in the house, and would report everything. But Jacob was not to be roused. He fought out with his fist at the unknown cause of disturbance, turned over, and snored again. He must be left to wake as he would. David, with a cold perspiration on his brow, confessed to himself that Jacob could not be got away that day.

Mr Palfrey came over to Grimworth before noon, with a natural curiosity to see how his future son-in-law got on with the stranger to whom he was so benevolently inclined. He found a crowd round the shop. All Grimworth by this time had heard how Freely had been fastened on by an idiot, who called him 'Brother Zavy;' and the younger population seemed to find the singular stranger an unwearying source of fascination, while the householders dropped in one by one to inquire into the incident.

'Why don't you send him to the workhouse?' said Mr Prettyman. 'You'll have a row with him and the children presently, and he'll eat you up. The workhouse is the proper place for him; let his kin claim him, if he's got any.'

'Those may be *your* feelings, Mr Prettyman,' said David, his mind quite enfeebled by the torture of his position.

'What! *is* he your brother, then?' said Mr Prettyman, looking at his neighbour Freely rather sharply.

'All men are our brothers, and idiots particular so,' said Mr Freely, who, like many other travelled men,[5] was not master of the English language.

'Come, come, if he's your brother, tell the truth, man,' said Mr Prettyman, with growing suspicion. 'Don't be ashamed of your own flesh and blood.'

Mr Palfrey was present, and also had his eye on Freely. It is difficult for a man to believe in the advantage of a truth which will disclose him to have been a liar. In this critical moment, David shrank from this immediate disgrace in the eyes of his future father-in-law.

'Mr Prettyman,' he said, 'I take your observations as an insult. I've no reason to be otherwise than proud of my own flesh and blood. If this poor man was my brother more than all men are, I should say so.'

A tall figure darkened the door, and David, lifting his eyes in that direction, saw his eldest brother, Jonathan, on the door-sill.

'I'll stay wi' Zavy,' shouted Jacob, as he, too, caught sight of his eldest brother; and, running behind the counter, he clutched David hard.

'What, he *is* here?' said Jonathan Faux, coming forward. 'My mother would have no nay, as he'd been away so long, but I must see after him. And it struck me he was very like come after you, because we'd been talking of you o' late, and where you lived.'

David saw there was no escape; he smiled a ghastly smile.

'What! is this a relation of yours, sir?' said Mr Palfrey to Jonathan.

'Ay, it's my innicent of a brother, sure enough,' said honest Jonathan. 'A fine trouble and cost he is to us, in th' eating and other things, but we must bear what's laid on us.'

'And your name's Freely, is it?' said Mr Prettyman.

'Nay, nay, my name's Faux, I know nothing o' Freelys,' said Jonathan, curtly. 'Come,' he added, turning to David, 'I must take some news to mother about Jacob. Shall I take him with me, or will you undertake to send him back?'

'Take him, if you can make him loose his hold of me,' said David, feebly.

'Is this gentleman here in the confectionery line your brother, then, sir?' said Mr Prettyman, feeling that it was an occasion on which formal language must be used.

'*I* don't want to own him,' said Jonathan, unable to resist a movement of indignation that had never been allowed to satisfy itself. 'He run away from home with good reasons in his pocket years ago: he didn't want to be owned again, I reckon.'

Mr Palfrey left the shop; he felt his own pride too severely wounded by the sense that he had let himself be fooled, to feel curiosity for further details. The most pressing business was to go home and tell his daughter that Freely was a poor sneak, probably a rascal, and that her engagement was broken off.

Mr Prettyman stayed, with some internal self-gratulation that *he* had never given in to Freely, and that Mr Chaloner would see now what sort of fellow it was that he had put over the heads of older parishioners. He considered it due from him (Mr Prettyman) that, for the interests of the parish, he should know all that was to be known about this 'interloper.' Grimworth would have people coming from Botany Bay[6] to settle in it, if things went on in this way.

It soon appeared that Jacob could not be made to quit his dear brother David except by force. He understood, with a clearness equal to that of the most intelligent mind, that Jonathan would take him back to skimmed milk, apple-dumpling, broad-beans, and pork. And he had found a paradise in his brother's shop. It was a difficult matter to use force with Jacob, for he wore heavy nailed boots; and if his pitchfork had been mastered, he would have resorted without hesitation to kicks. Nothing short of using guile to bind him hand and foot would have made all parties safe.

'Let him stay,' said David, with desperate resignation, frightened above all things at the idea of further disturbances in his shop, which would make his exposure all the more conspicuous. '*You* go away again, and to-morrow I can, perhaps, get him to go to Gilsbrook with me. He'll follow me fast enough, I daresay,' he added, with a half-groan.

'Very well,' said Jonathan, gruffly. 'I don't see why *you* shouldn't have some trouble and expense with him as well as the rest of us. But mind you bring him back safe and soon, else mother'll never rest.'

On this arrangement being concluded, Mr Prettyman begged Mr Jonathan Faux to go and take a snack with him, an invitation which was quite acceptable; and as honest Jonathan had nothing to be ashamed of, it is probable that he was very frank in his communications to the civil draper, who, pursuing the benefit of the parish, hastened to make all the information he could gather about Freely common parochial property. You may imagine that the meeting of the Club at the Woolpack that evening was unusually lively. Every member was anxious to prove that he had never liked Freely, as he called himself. Faux was his name, was it? Fox would have been more suitable. The majority expressed a desire to see him hooted out of the town.

Mr Freely did not venture over his door-sill that day, for he knew Jacob would keep at his side, and there was every probability that they would have a train of juvenile followers. He sent to engage the Woolpack gig for an early hour the next morning; but this order was not kept religiously a secret by the landlord. Mr Freely was informed that he could not have the gig till seven; and the Grimworth people were early risers. Perhaps they were more alert than usual on this particular morning ; for when Jacob, with a bag of sweets in his hand, was induced to mount the gig with his brother David, the inhabitants of the market-place were looking out of their doors and windows, and at the turning of the street there was even a muster of apprentices and schoolboys, who shouted as they passed in what Jacob took to be a very merry and friendly way, nodding and grinning in return. 'Huzzay, David Faux! how's your uncle?' was their morning's greeting. Like other pointed things, it was not altogether impromptu.

Even this public derision was not so crushing to David as the horrible thought that though he might succeed now in getting Jacob home again there would never be any security against his coming back, like a wasp to the honey-pot. As long as David lived at Grimworth, Jacob's return would be hanging over him. But could he go on living at Grimworth – an object of ridicule, discarded by the Palfreys, after having revelled in the consciousness that he was an envied and prosperous confectioner? David liked to be envied; he minded less about being loved.

His doubts on this point were soon settled. The mind of Grimworth became obstinately set against him and his viands, and the new school being finished, the eating-room was closed. If there had been no other reason, sympathy with the Palfreys, that respectable family who had lived in the parish time out of mind, would have determined all well-to-do people to decline Freely's goods. Besides, he had absconded with his mother's guineas: who knew what else he had done, in Jamaica or elsewhere, before he came to Grimworth, worming himself into families under false pretences? Females shuddered. Dreadful suspicions gathered round him: his green eyes, his bow-legs, had a criminal aspect. The rector disliked the sight of a man who had imposed upon him; and all boys who could not afford to purchase, hooted 'David Faux' as they passed his shop. Certainly no man now would pay anything for the 'goodwill' of Mr Freely's business, and he would be obliged to quit it without a peculium[7] so desirable towards defraying the expense of moving.

In a few months the shop in the market-place was again to let, and Mr David Faux, *alias* Mr Edward Freely, had gone – nobody at Grimworth knew whither. In this way the demoralisation of Grimworth women was checked. Young Mrs Steene renewed her efforts to make light mince-pies, and having at last made a batch so excellent that Mr Steene looked at her with complacency as he ate them, and said they were the best he had ever eaten in his life, she thought less of bulbuls and renegades ever after. The secrets of the finer cookery were revived in the breasts of matronly housewives, and daughters were again anxious to be initiated in them.

You will further, I hope, be glad to hear, that some purchases of drapery made by pretty Penny, in preparation for her marriage with Mr Freely, came in quite as well for her wedding with young Towers as if they had been made expressly for the latter occasion. For Penny's complexion had not altered, and blue always became it best.

Here ends the story of Mr David Faux, confectioner, and his brother Jacob. And we see in it, I think, an admirable instance of the unexpected forms in which the great Nemesis[8] hides herself.

(1860.)

The Lifted Veil

TITLE

George Eliot's original working title was 'The Hidden Veil', which seems almost a contradiction in terms. The more apposite 'Lifted' draws on ideas of lifting the veil of truth, frequently employed by George Henry Lewes in his science writing (see Introduction), and the veil of death, as in Tennyson's *In Memoriam* (1850): 'What hope of answer, or redress? Behind the veil, behind the veil' (LVI, 27–8). There is also probably an echo of Shelley's famous sonnet (1824): 'Lift not the painted veil which those who live/Call Life . . .'

EPIGRAPH

1. This was added for the Cabinet edition of 1878. Eliot had composed it on rereading the tale in 1873. See Introduction, 'Resurrection'.

CHAPTER I

1. *angina pectoris*: This is a highly appropriate disease for Latimer. It was first defined by Dr William Heberden (1710-1801) in 1768 who named it on account of its physical location in the chest, and 'the sense of strangling anxiety with which it is attended'. Mid-nineteenth-century accounts went even further in stressing the mental qualities of the disease: 'There seems to be something peculiar in the pain, whatever be its degree . . . as if it were combined with something of a *mental* quality. There is a feeling and a fear of impending death; and the primary symptoms of corporeal disorder are speedily modified by the consequences of mental impressions conveyed through the nervous system' (John Forbes, 'Angina Pectoris', in John Forbes, Alexander Tweedie and John Conolly (eds.), *Cyclopaedia of Practical Medicine*, 4 vols. (London: Sherwood, Gilbert and Piper, 1833), I, 82). Latimer's sense of impending death is thus given

a firm medical grounding, with the additional suggestion that his fears of death actually contribute to his demise.

2. *ubi sæva . . . nequit*: Where savage indignation can no longer tear the heart (Latin). Part of the epitaph Swift composed for himself, drawing on Juvenal, *Satire* I. 79: 'si natura negat, facit indignatio versum' ('though natural endowment forbids, indignation makes the poem').

3. *missed my mother's love*: Eliot's mother had died when she was sixteen. There are various parallels between Eliot's own situation and that of Latimer: her mother was also a second wife, whom Robert Evans married at the age of forty.

4. *those dead but sceptred spirits*: Misquotation of Byron's Manfred (1817): 'The dead but sceptred sovereigns, who still rule/ Our spirits from their urns' (III, iv).

5. *Potter's 'Æschylus' . . . Francis's 'Horace'*: Standard school texts dating from the eighteenth century, but continually republished during the nineteenth: Robert Potter, *The Tragedies of Aeschylus* (1777), and the Revd Philip Francis, *A Poetical Translation of the Works of Horace* (1743–6).

6. *mining speculations*: It is unclear whether Latimer's father was opening up mining on his own land, or investing in the mines now increasingly being opened by the aristocracy and gentry on their lands. There was a growing pressure at this period for the reform of school and university education to include natural sciences.

7. *Mr Letherall*: A fictional exponent of the science of phrenology, first theorized by Franz Joseph Gall (1758–1828) at the turn of the century, but popularized in England primarily by George Combe, from the late 1820s onwards, in *The Constitution of Man* (1828) and various phrenological handbooks. Combe taught that the size and strength of the various faculties of the mind could be discerned through measuring the contours of the skull. Harmful propensities could then be suppressed by education, and weak faculties developed. The faculties or organs which lie around the eyebrows (and hence Latimer's weak points, or areas of deficiency) are the perceptive ones of Form, Size, Weight, Colouring, Locality, Number, Order, Time. Latimer has an excess, around the sides of the head, of Hope, Wonder, Ideality. His scientific education would thus attempt to overcome his weaknesses, and control his 'excess' of artistic tendencies. Eliot had an early interest in phrenology and had a cast taken of her head in 1844. For her friendship with George Combe and later attitude to phrenology, see Introduction and notes 42 and 48.

8. *academy*: The following was deleted from the *Blackwood's* text: 'whence I have been led to conclude that the only universal rule with regard to education is, that no rule should be held universal, a good education being that which adapts itself to individual wants and faculties'.

9. *Plutarch . . . and Don Quixote*: Plutarch (*c. 50–c.* 120), Greek prose writer, whose

most important works include *Parallel Lives* which portrays noble deeds and characters from Greek and Roman times, and the *Moralia* or *Ethica*, a series of more than sixty essays on ethical, religious, political and literary topics. *Don Quixote* by Miguel de Cervantes (1547–1616), was published in two parts in 1605 and 1615.

10. *uncongenial medium*: Eliot shared Lewes's scientific concern with the inter-action between organism and medium, a principle that defined equally, they believed, the processes of physiological or social life. See Eliot's essay 'The Natural History of German Life' (1856; *Essays*, p. 287).

11. *Geneva*: Eliot had gone to Geneva after her father died in June 1849, lodging first at Plongeon, and then until March 1850 with the portrait painter François D'Albert-Durade and his wife, who became her close friends. Her responses to the landscape were similar to those of Latimer. See *Letters*, I, 329 ('If you saw the Jura today!') and I, 302:

This place looks more lovely to me every day – the lake, the town, the campagnes with their stately trees and pretty houses, the glorious mountains in the distance – one can hardly believe one's self on earth – one might live here and forget that there is such a thing as want or labour or sorrow. The perpetual presence of all this beauty has somewhat the effect of mesmerism or chloroform. I feel sometimes as if I were sinking into an agreeable state of numbness on the verge of unconsciousness and seem to want well pinching to rouse me.

12. *Jean Jacques*: Jean-Jacques Rousseau (1712–78), Geneva-born social theorist and novelist who had a profound effect on theorists of the French Revolution and on the development of Romantic literary sensibilities. In 1848 Eliot identi-fied his *Confessions* as the work which had first stimulated her to deep reflection (see *Letters*, I, 271 n. 6; and also I, 277). Book 12 of the *Confessions* contains Rousseau's account of rowing on the lake:

Often, letting my boat drift with the wind and the current, I gave myself up to aimless dreams which, foolish though they were, were none the less delightful. Sometimes I cried out with emotion: 'O Nature! O my mother! I am here under your sole protection. Here there is no cunning and rascally man to thrust himself between us.' In this way I would drift almost a mile and a half from land; and I could have wished that lake were the ocean. (trans. J. M. Cohen (Harmondsworth: Penguin, 1953), p. 594)

Hugh Witemeyer suggests in 'George Eliot and Jean-Jacques Rousseau', *Comparative Literature Studies* 16 (1979), pp. 121–30, that there are strong similarities in personality and outlook between Rousseau and Latimer. Unlike Rousseau, however, Latimer was never able to harness his emotional energies creatively.

13. *the prophet's chariot of fire*: Elijah's chariot, see 2 Kings 2: 11: 'there appeared a chariot of fire, and horses of fire, and parted them [Elijah and Elisha] both

asunder; and Elijah went up by a whirlwind into heaven' (Authorized Version).

14. *Meunier*: Gordon Haight suggests that Eliot took the name from a celebrated preacher whom she used to hear in Geneva (*George Eliot: A Biography* (Oxford: Oxford University Press, 1968), p. 74).

15. *gamins*: Street boys or urchins.

16. *the Salève . . . to Vevay*: The Petit Salève (2962 ft) about 5 miles south-east of Geneva. Murray's *Handbook for Travellers in Switzerland* (London: John Murray and Son, 1838) notes that a steamboat ran from Geneva to ports on the northern shore of the lake, including Vevay, taking about 7 or 8 hours. Eliot had climbed the Salève and visited Vevay in 1849. See *Letters*, I, 319.

17. *Latimer*: It is unclear why Eliot chose this name. His most famous namesake would be Hugh Latimer (*c.* 1485–1555), martyr of the English Reformation, who was burned at the stake with Nicholas Ridley in front of Balliol College in 1855. If this is the provenance, the name would work by opposition, since Hugh Latimer was not simply a martyr in his own imaginings. In *Middlemarch*, Lydgate praises Mr Farebrother as a kind of Latimer: 'I never heard such good preaching as his – such plain, easy eloquence. He would have done to preach at St Paul's Cross after old Latimer. His talk is just as good about all subjects: original, simple, clear. I think him a remarkable fellow' (Bk. 5, ch. 50). Eliot's Latimer is remarkable, but for exactly the opposite qualities; he is non-communicative, and lacks all faith, whether in himself, in others, or God.

18. *gold-inwoven . . . unending bridge*: A possible echo of Alexander Pope, 'Odyssey' (1725–6), IV, 406: 'Rich tapestry, stiff with inwoven gold'. The Carlsbrücke spans the Moldau; it was constructed by Charles IV in the fourteenth century. Each side is decorated with twenty-eight statues of saints. Eliot visited Prague with Lewes in August 1858, and noted in her journal:

After dinner we took a carriage and went across the wonderful bridge of St. Jean Nepomuck with its avenue of statues, towards the Radschin – an ugly straight-lined building but grand in effect from its magnificent site, on the summit of an eminence crowded with old massive buildings. The view from this eminence is one of the most impressive in the world – perhaps as much from one's associations with Prague as from its visible grandeur and antiquity. (*Journals*, p. 324).

St Jean Nepomuck was one of the saints depicted on the bridge. A few lines later Latimer's 'palace' is the Hradschin, or Radschin.

19. *draught*: Liquid medicine.

20. *humiliated . . . nightmare*: Latimer clearly follows Romantic beliefs that the qualities of dreams are indicative of the subject's imaginary powers. Dreams and nightmares were much debated in nineteenth-century psychology. Robert Macnish, in his influential *The Philosophy of Sleep* (1830), notes that certain diseases such as angina pectoris are apt to induce nightmare, and asks: 'Why

are literary men, deep thinkers, and hypochondriacs peculiarly subject to nightmare?' (*Embodied Selves: An Anthology of Psychological Texts, 1830–1890*, ed. Jenny Bourne Taylor and Sally Shuttleworth (Oxford: Oxford University Press, 1998), pp. 102–6).

21. *dissolving view*: Technique for displaying magic-lantern slides, invented in the early decades of the nineteenth century, whereby one scene could be made to 'dissolve' into another.

22. *Homer . . . Dante . . . Milton*: Homer's *Iliad* (ninth century BC), Dante's *Divine Comedy* (1300–18) and Milton's *Paradise Lost* (1667). Latimer is not content with comparing his vision to that of minor poets, but chooses the three great epic writers who have defined the western literary tradition. All were writers whose works Eliot knew intimately, and returned to again and again. She had been reading Milton's 'Samson Agonistes' at the time of writing 'The Lifted Veil' (*Lewes Ms Journal* X, 20 March 1859).

23. *Novalis*: Pen name of Friedrich Leopold, Baron von Hardenberg (1772–1801), German Romantic poet and novelist who died of consumption. His last years during his illness were astonishingly productive. Latimer would no doubt have been drawn to his mythical romance *Heinrich von Ofterdingen* (1802), which describes the mystical and romantic searchings of a young poet. Novalis also figures in *The Mill on the Floss* (Bk. 6, ch. 6).

24. *Canaletto*: Giovanni Canaletto (1697–1768), Italian painter who produced unrivalled imaginative and dramatic interpretations of Venetian architecture. In 1741–4 he expanded his range to include a series of thirty etchings.

25. *Water-Nixie*: Water sprite who lured men to their deaths. Eliot had written an article on 'German Mythology and Legend' for the *Leader* 7 (1855), pp. 917–18. Lewes had translated Goethe's ballad, 'The Fisherman', which recounts how a fisherman is fatally seduced by such a sprite, in his *Life and Works of Goethe*, 2 vols. (London: David Nutt, 1855), I, 367–8.

26. *Monsieur ne se trouve pas bien*: Are you feeling unwell, Sir? (French). Pierre responds below 'Bien' – Very well.

27. *Hôtel des Bergues*: The foremost hotel in Geneva. Murray's *Handbook for Travellers in Switzerland* notes: 'Hotel des Bergues, a grand establishment, recently built, facing the lake – expensive.'

28. *Bertha*: Eliot possibly drew the name Bertha from Mary Shelley's story 'The Mortal Immortal' (1834) where the narrator, who yearns to die, but cannot commit suicide, is tormented by his love for a wealthy, teasing coquette named Bertha. See Sandra M. Gilbert and Susan Gubar, *The Madwoman in the Attic: The Woman Writer and the Nineteenth-Century Literary Imagination* (New Haven: Yale University Press, 1979), p. 458.

29. *prevision*: Mesmerism had claimed powers of prevision for its subjects, and although mainstream psychology had dismissed the more outlandish claims,

there was a strong interest in how 'sentiments of pre-existence', as A. L. Wigan defined them in *The Duality of Mind* (London: Longman, Brown, Green and Longman, 1844), could physiologically occur. John Draper in *Human Physiology* (London: Sampson Low, Son and Co., 1856), a work Eliot diligently read out loud to Lewes in the evenings in 1857 (*Letters*, II, 369), disputed Wigan's account and gave examples from his own life to suggest that incidents could be experienced over and over again. The sentiment of pre-existence, he noted, is 'that strange impression, which all persons have occasionally observed in the course of their lives, that some incident or scene at the moment occurring to them, it may be of a quite trivial nature, has been witnessed by them once before, and is in an instant recognised' (p. 331). See also Introduction, 'Prevision'.

30. *fancy picture*: Form of picture, popularized by Van Dyck in England, where a sitter is painted as an historical or allegorical figure. See Hugh Witemeyer, *George Eliot and the Visual Arts* (New Haven: Yale University Press, 1979), pp. 92–3, 212–13. On her visit to the Lichtenstein Palace in Vienna in 1858 Eliot had admired Van Dyck's portraits, 'especially the pale delicate face of Wallenstein, with blue eyes and pale auburn locks' (*Journals*, p. 323). (D'Albert-Durade's portrait of Eliot, painted during her stay in Geneva, now hangs in the National Portrait Gallery, London.)

31. *affinity*: *Blackwood's* text had the less apposite 'sympathy'.

32. *German lyrics*: I.e. German Romantic lyrics. Eliot was particularly interested in the work of Heine, who formed the subject of three of her articles. In 'German Wit: Heinrich Heine' (*Westminster Review*, 45 (January 1856)), she praised his *Buch der Lieder* (*Book of Songs*): 'a volume of lyrics, of which it is hard to say whether their greatest charm is the lightness and finish of their style, their vivid and original imaginativeness, or their simple, pure sensibility' (*Essays*, p. 233).

33. *sylphs . . . bonne et brave femme*: Slender and graceful young women or girls, derived from the original meaning of spirits of the air. French: good and worthy woman (and by implication, not attractive).

34. *feminine*: 'slight feminine' in the *Blackwood's* text.

35. *opal*: Stone whose colours appear to change with varying lights. Opals were traditionally associated with bad luck.

36. *preternaturally heightened sense of hearing*: See Introduction, 'Diseased vision'.

37. *energumen*: One possessed by the devil, or unnatural powers. See also *Romola*: Bk. I, ch. 5.

38. *Lichtenberg Palace*: A mistake for the Lichtenstein Palace, visited by Eliot and Lewes in 1858.

39. *Lucrezia Borgia*: Eliot had admired this picture on her visit to the Belvedere Gallery, noting that 'Titian's Danae was one that delighted us: besides this I remember Giorgione's Lucrezia Borgia with the cruel, cruel eyes' (*Journals*,

p. 323). It was described in Murray's *Handbook for Continental Travellers* as 'Lucretia Borgia regarding a sketch of Lucretia, with an inscription'. The attribution to Giorgione was later determined to be an error, and the painting is now thought to have been a copy of Lorenzo Lotto's *A Lady as Lucretia*. (c. 1533), now in the National Gallery, London (Helen Small (ed.), *The Lifted Veil and Brother Jacob*, Oxford World's Classics (Oxford, 1999). Ironically, the new attribution links the figure in the painting not to the infamous Lucrezia Borgia, but to the virtuous Roman lady Lucretia who committed suicide after being raped and had become a traditional symbol for chastity. The painting, however, wittily plays with these associations, placing the sitter's actual chastity in question.

40. *Belvedere Gallery*: Housed in the Belvedere Palace, and holding the Imperial Picture Gallery.

41. *Grand Terrace*: Eliot and Lewes had visited the Belvedere Terrace: 'The next morning, we had a view of the town from the Belvedere Terrace, St. Stephen's sending its exquisite tower aloft from among an almost level forest of houses and inconspicuous churches' (*Journals*, p. 323).

42. *dogs*: Andirons, usually made of iron or brass and placed either side of a fireplace to support the burning wood.

43. *The dying Cleopatra*: The Cleopatra motif is picked up in the vision of Bertha which fades to an image of a green serpent. The associations align Cleopatra with the treacherous water-nixies who lure men to their doom. In Shakespeare's *Antony and Cleopatra* Cleopatra is known as the serpent of the Nile. Having brought about the death of Antony, she dies by placing an asp to her breast.

44. *girl*: Emphasis added for the Cabinet edition.

45. *an old story*: The most famous version was the legend of Faust, retold by Goethe in his verse drama *Faustus* (1810–32).

46. *impulse . . . savage*: *Blackwood's* text: with no less savage an impulse.

47. *patent tram-road*: Initially used in the early nineteenth century for a narrow track for wagons or cars (particularly in collieries), and later for railways, as distinct from tramways which ran on suburban streets. The first Stockton to Darlington line (1825) was known as a railway or tramroad.

48. *thorny wilderness*: In the Old Testament where the Israelites were led by Moses after their exodus from Egypt. They remained in the wilderness for forty years. See also note 12 to ch. 2 of 'Brother Jacob'.

49. *double consciousness*: Term drawn from contemporary physiological psychology, and linked to research into the double hemispheres of the brain. The physician, Henry Holland, had written an essay 'On the Brain as a Double Organ' in 1840, which was followed by Wigan's *The Duality of Mind* (see note 29 above). Holland's most influential contribution to the debate was the section in *Chapters on Mental Physiology* (London: Longman, Brown, Green and

Longman, 1852) where he defines double consciousness as a state in which 'the mind passes by alternation from one state to another, each having the perception of external impressions and appropriate trains of thought, but not linked together by the ordinary gradations, or by mutual memory' (p. 198). Eliot was certainly aware of Holland's work through Lewes. Draper's *Human Physiology* includes an extended discussion of the double action of the brain and Wigan's theories, and notes that the insane can have two independent trains of thought, and 'in this case doubleness of thought is seen in its most exaggerated aspect, but in a less degree, it may be remarked, in the thinking operations of those whose minds are perfectly sound' (p. 329). For extracts from Wigan, Holland and other contributors to the double consciousness debate, see Taylor and Shuttleworth (eds.), *Embodied Selves*, pp. 123–40.

50. *flatter ourselves. We try*: *Blackwood's* text has 'flatter ourselves, trying'.

51. *hemmed in . . . our egoism*: Eliot reworked this passage for the Cabinet edition. The *Blackwood's* text read: 'hindered our generosity, our awe, our human piety, from flooding our hard cruel indifference to the sensations and feelings of our fellow, with the tenderness and self-renunciation which have only come when the egoism has had its day'.

52. *Jewish cicerone*: See Eliot's description of her visit to the Prague synagogue in 1858: 'Then came the sombre old synagogue with its smoked groins, and lamp for ever burning. An intelligent Jew was our cicerone [guide] and read us some Hebrew out of the precious old book of the Law' (*Journals*, p. 324).

CHAPTER 2

1. *our own emotions take the form of a drama*: In *The Mill on the Floss*: '[Maggie's] own life was still a drama for her, in which she demanded of herself that her part should be played with intensity' (Bk. IV, ch. 3).

2. *ménage*: Household (French).

3. *Tasso*: Torquato Tasso (1544–95), author of *Gerusalemme Liberata* (1575). In 1576 he showed the first signs of mental disorder, becoming suspicious and melancholy, and convinced there were plots to assassinate him. In 1579 he was confined as insane at Ferrara, by order of the Duke of Ferrara (Alphonso d'Este II); he continued to write until his growing fame led to intercessions on his behalf and he was released in 1586. For the Romantic poets he became a paradigm of the suffering artist, an image intensified by the mistaken belief, perpetuated in Byron's 'Lament of Tasso' (1817), that he had been confined due to his love for the Princess Leonora.

4. *syren melody*: The sirens, in Greek mythology, lured men to destruction by

their singing. Odysseus had his men's ears filled with wax, and bound himself to the mast so that they could sail past the sirens unharmed.

5. *stood for the borough*: stood for election as a Member of Parliament.

6. *hashish*: Indian hemp. Herbert Spencer had noted in *Principles of Psychology* (London: Longman, Brown, Green and Longman, 1855) that hashish was well known to give an excessive vividness to the sensations. Its effects were much debated in nineteenth-century psychology. Lewes, for example, possessed an 1847 review article of J. Moreau, *Psychological Studies on Hachisch and on Mental Derangement.*

7. *the pale hues*: *Blackwood's* text has 'the pale sunshine'.

8. *crack-brained*: Crazy, or with intellect impaired.

9. *incubus*: Evil demon, or oppressive presence, that weighs upon the sufferer. Commonly used of nightmares. Henry Fuseli's famous painting, *The Nightmare* (1790–91), shows a form of incubus, or familiar spirit, of semi-animal form crouched on a woman's chest (see also note 11).

10. *We learn words by rote*: In reworking this material in *Daniel Deronda* Eliot returned to the question of language's failure to represent adequately. Mordecai notes that he could, if he wished, 'silence the beliefs which are the mother-tongue of my soul and speak with the rote-learned language of a system, that gives you the spelling of all things, sure of its alphabet covering them all' (Bk. III, ch. 27).

11. *familiar demon*: Evil spirit, under the individual's command, often appearing in animal form. See also *Daniel Deronda*, where Grandcourt conquers Gwendolen: 'No familar spirit could have suggested to him more effective words' (Bk. III, ch. 27).

12. *a clairvoyant*: Person with the power of seeing into the future. The term was introduced into England in the nineteenth century in a specific mesmeric context, but quickly broadened to refer more generally to powers of insight. Latimer is no doubt bitter against the various mesmeric practitioners who claimed similar powers to his own. Lewes had written an article attacking mesmerism, 'The Fallacy of Clairvoyance', in the *Leader* (27 March 1852).

13. *peritonitis*: Inflammation of the lining of the abdomen. In the nineteenth century it was deemed to be one of the most painful things that a person could suffer.

14. *transfusing blood*: Transfusion had been carried out in France in the late seventeenth century, initially on animals, but then a madman was infused with the blood of a calf and pronounced cured. Further experiments were banned, however, after several deaths, but the idea was taken up again in the early nineteenth century by James Blundell, and subsequently by Brown-Séquard. Lewes gives the history of transfusion in 'Blood', *Blackwood's Edinburgh Magazine* 83 (June 1858), pp. 698–9. He draws his details mainly from P. Bérard's *Cours*

de Physiologie (1851), which gives numerous accounts of nineteenth-century transfusions which took place primarily for women who had undergone childbirth, and where the blood was usually drawn from the husband. See also Introduction, 'Resurrection'. Lewes, in rewriting his discussion of transfusions for *The Physiology of Common Life* (Edinburgh and London: William Blackwood, 1859), included the observation that transfusions are of use only when there is a dangerous loss of blood: 'In all cases of disease it is useless, or worse' (I, 277). One might speculate that this new caution in Lewes's approach perhaps stemmed from discussions stimulated by the publication of 'The Lifted Veil'.

15. *peignoir*: Loose dressing-gown.

16. *artificial respiration*: The precise technique used by Latimer is unclear: see Introduction, note 72.

17. *Great God! Is this what it is to live again*: *Blackwood's* text, 'Good God! This is what it is to live again!' The later version, with its question format, moves us outward from Latimer's narrow consciousness, to all readers.

Brother Jacob

EPIGRAPH

1. *Trompeurs . . . la pareille*: Deceivers, I write for you, Expect a similar fate: from La Fontaine's fable of 'The Fox and the Stork' (1668). Eliot frequently drew on La Fontaine's fables in her work, and had concluded her essay 'Silly Novels by Lady Novelists' (1856) with a fable of the ass, ridiculing false confidence in one's own creative powers (*Essays*, p. 324). As Peter Allan Dale points out, 'Brother Jacob' adopts the generic form of a fable. Lewes, he also notes, was similarly preoccupied with fables at this time ('George Eliot's "Brother Jacob"; fables and the physiology of common life', *Philological Quarterly* 64 (1985), pp. 32–3).

CHAPTER I

1. *yeoman*: Small landholder, more generally a respectable countryman.

2. *confectioner*: In her 'Recollections of Weimar' (1854) Eliot recalls that her landlady's husband was called 'sweet' Münderloh,

by way of distinction from his brother who was the reverse of sweet. This Münderloh who was *not* sweet – but who nonetheless dealt in sweets – in other words was a confectioner, was so utter a rogue that any transaction with him was dreaded almost as if he had been the devil himself, and so *clever* a rogue that he always managed to keep on the windy side of the law.

Eliot notes that people 'bent on fine entertainment' felt they had to use his wares, 'And so he got custom in spite of general detestation' (*Journals*, p. 221). This figure no doubt supplies part of the inspiration for David Faux.

3. *marengs ... twelfth-cake*: Meringues, and an iced-cake, baked for Twelfth Night, and usually hiding a bean or coin; the finder would be king or queen of the festivities.

4. *doctrine of the Inconceivable*: Refers to an ongoing contemporary debate about the nature of truth in which Herbert Spencer played a leading role. On 9 July 1853, Lewes had written to Spencer thanking him for the proofs of his article on the Universal Postulate: 'I have read it with immense interest and think you make out an irresistible case against Hamilton, Hume, Kant & Co' (*Letters*, VIII, 76). Spencer argued that

a belief which is proved by the invariableness of its negation to invariably exist, is true. We have seen that this is the assumption on which every conclusion whatever ultimately rests. We have no other guarantee for the reality of consciousness, of sensations, of personal existence; we have no other guarantee for any other axiom; we have no other guarantee for any step in a demonstration. Hence, as being taken for granted in every act of understanding, it must be regarded as the *Universal Postulate*. (*Westminster Review* 60 (October 1853), pp. 513–50)

Eliot had been involved in the writing of this article (*Letters*, II, 145). The debate, which also involved John Stuart Mill, continued through the 1850s, and had most recently been added to by William Hamilton in his *Lectures on Metaphysics and Logic* (1859–60), which features extensively in Lewes's *Physiology of Common Life*.

The danger of an 'initial mistake' in career choice which undermined the subsequent reception of high intellectual endeavour was shown in the cases of Spencer, who started life as a railway engineer, and even more markedly for Lewes, who was a novelist, literary critic and theatrical performer, before turning to science. In 1859 he was still struggling hard to gain acceptance within the English scientific community as a fully fledged scientist.

5. *drop-cakes ... sugar department*: Drop-cakes are cooked on a griddle; *sugar department*: the *Cornhill* text has 'suck department'.

6. *Mechanics' Institute*: Established by George Birkbeck in Glasgow and London in the early 1820s, and swiftly copied in small towns and cities across England. The aim was to offer the means of education and self-improvement for the working man. The Institutes held lecture series and classes, usually on scientific topics, and ran their own libraries.

7. *'Inkle and Yarico'*: For a summary of the story and its publication, see Introduction, 'Brother Jacob'. The story was based on an account in *A True and Exact History of the Island of Barbadoes* by Richard Ligon (1673). Steele invented the name Inkle, and the detail about Yarico's pregnancy. The numerous subsequent adaptations of the story include George Colman Jr's musical play *Inkle and Yarico* (1787), which rewrote the ending so that Inkle is re-converted to Christian charity and does right by Yarico. Even if David possesses a copy of this later version, as a character he is clearly more in sympathy with the original.

8. below a certain mark: The *Cornhill* text was more scathing: 'below a mark'.

9. *beans*: Goods; from the French, *biens*.

10. *Chubb's patent*: Charles Chubb (1773–1845) took out his first patent for a Chubb lock in 1818, establishing a far safer system of securing buildings and valuables.

11. *Sally*: Sally Lunn shares her name with that of an iced bun.

12. *mens nil conscia sibi*: A mind with no consciousness of guilt (Latin). There is no exact classical parallel, thus possibly adding to the humour of the reference to the learned friend. Eliot could be thinking either of Aeneas' Address to Dido, *Aeneid* I. 604: 'mens sibi conscia recti' (a mind conscious of rectitude); or of Horace on the importance of maintaining a clear conscience: 'Nil conscire sibi' (literally, 'to know nothing against oneself'), which is closer in meaning to the context. Lewes was working at this time on the subjectivity of perception, and the ways in which 'background Consciousness' determined our perception even of physical objects (see *The Physiology of Common Life*, II, 68).

13. *jujubes*: Lozenges flavoured with imitation berry juice.

14. *Louis Napoleon*: Charles Louis Napoleon Bonaparte (1808–73), nephew of Napoleon I and Emperor of France (1852–70). In order to seize power he dissolved the Constitution in December 1851, and imprisoned and deported opponents.

15. *Caliban . . . Trinculo's wine*: In *The Tempest*, the semi-bestial figure of Caliban swears he will be the lowly Trinculo's devoted subject, once having tasted his 'celestial liquor' (II, ii).

16. *psychology of idiots*: This was a highly topical area of study in 1860. The first purpose-built asylum for idiots had been established in England in 1853, and, following the work of Dr Guggenbühl in Switzerland, and Samuel Gridley Howe in Massachusetts, attempts were made to educate the inmates. Psychological texts for the first time started to explore the mental states of idiocy. In 1859 Eliot and Lewes read J. Moreau, *La Psychologie Morbide* (1859), which contained extensive discussions of idiocy (*Letters*, III, 149–50).

17. *day-mare*: Waking nightmare.

18. *sweet-tasted fetish*: Figure to be worshipped. The founder of positivism, Auguste Comte (1798–1857), argued that fetishism was the first form of belief

system in primitive societies. See also *The Mill on the Floss* where Maggie Tulliver beats her fetish (Bk. I, ch. 4) and Introduction, 'The Idiot Brother'.

19. *host*: Possibly used in the new biological sense, where David would then be parasite to Jacob's host.

20. *heroes of M. de Balzac*: Eliot had recently read Honoré de Balzac's *Eugénie Grandet* (1833) (entry for 6 June 1859, *Lewes Ms Journal*) and *Le Père Goriot* (1834) which, contrary to her usual enthusiasm for Balzac, she described as 'a hateful book' (25 October 1859; *Journals*, p. 81). Eliot was probably thinking of the latter, particularly the figure of Vautrin who advocates a similar philosophy of self-interest to that held by David Faux, and predicts the future of various characters, claiming fortune-telling powers.

21. *openings – even for cats*: Cats were imported into the West Indies and other colonies to keep down the rodent populations.

22. *'duly set'*: From 'Robin Good-fellow' in *Percy's Reliques* (1767):

> Tells how the drudging Goblin swet
> To earn his cream-bowle duly set ...' (XXIV)

23. *calculate consequences ... virtue*: The utilitarian philosopher Jeremy Bentham (1748–1832) argued in *Introduction to the Principles of Morals and Legislation* (1789) that the proper objective of all conduct and legislation is 'the greatest happiness of the greatest number' and had outlined the 'felicific calculus' to help estimate the consequences of actions.

24. *The ways ... pleasantness*: Ironic rewriting of the description of wisdom in Proverbs 3:17: 'Her ways are ways of pleasantness, and all her paths are peace.'

25. *Gorgon or Demogorgon*: The Gorgons, in classical mythology, were three sisters with snakes for hair. Anyone who gazed on them was turned to stone. The Demogorgon first appears in the fourth century, as the primeval god of ancient mythology; the very mention of his name was meant to bring death and disaster.

CHAPTER 2

1. *Church-people ... Dissenters*: The division is between those who attend the established Church of England, and those who follow a whole range of Nonconformist religious practices, including Methodists, Baptists, Congregationalists, Quakers and Unitarians. As this comic representation suggests, the divisions were not merely religious, but also social and cultural.

2. *Zephaniah Crypt's Charity*: The given name, drawn from one of the Old Testament prophets, marks this as a dissenting charity. As befits his namesake's surname, Zephaniah was a prophet of gloom and doom.

3. *Yellow Coat School*: Charity schools traditionally clothed their pupils in coloured garments so that they could be easily identified. The most famous uniform was that of Christ's Hospital, London, where the pupils wore blue gowns and bright yellow stockings. 'Yellow hammer' was the nickname for charity school boys in yellow breeches.

4. *China-asters*: Daisy-like flower related to the Michaelmas daisy. The concern relates to the new development of stylish window-dressing, creating an imaginative lure for customers.

5. *jobbed linen*: Obviously a pejorative description, suggesting either that the work had been put out as a job to various hands, or bought as a 'job-lot' with a view to profit.

6. *shutters were taken down*: Wooden shutters on shop windows were usually detachable, and taken down in the morning and replaced each evening. Hinged iron shutters were introduced in the 1830s, but both systems continued through the century.

7. *collared and marbled meats*: *Collared* meats were usually pickled, and then boiled, boned and pressed into a roll. *Marbled* meats would have had fine veins of fat showing in the lean portions, a sign of quality.

8. *Dutch painter*: In *Adam Bede* Eliot had defined her art in relation to Dutch painting which caught the play of light and colour in the lives of ordinary folk:

> It is for this rare, precious quality of truthfulness that I delight in many Dutch paintings ... I turn, without shrinking, from cloud-borne angels, from prophets, sibyls, and heroic warriors, to an old woman bending over her flower-pot, or eating her solitary dinner, while the noonday light, softened perhaps by a screen of leaves, falls on her mob-cap, and just touches the rim of her spinning-wheel, and her stone jug. (ch. 17)

9. *Turner's latest style*: The precise reference cannot be pinpointed, but Eliot is probably referring either to the change in the style of J. M. W. Turner (1775–1871) after his first visit to Italy, which resulted in works which show a subordination of topography to the effects of light and colour, such as *Venice; Looking East from the Giudecca, Sunrise* (1819), or that which occurred after his second visit to Italy in 1828–9 when he started to use more brilliant colours, as in *Ulysses Deriding Polyphemus* (1829), which one critic considered as 'a specimen of colouring run mad' (Homan Potterton, *The National Gallery, London* (London: Thames and Hudson, 1977), p. 149).

10. *Punch ... tabernacle*: The booth for a Punch and Judy puppet show. Since 'tabernacle' was usually employed in a religious sense, and had become the term for Nonconformist sites of worship, Eliot is possibly playing on these associations to suggest an alternate form of worship for the young folk of Grimworth.

11. *mazarine*: Deep rich blue.

12. *manna-gift*: The food miraculously supplied by God for the Israelites in their wanderings through the wilderness: Exodus 16:15.

13. *missionaries ... negro's discontent*: The slave-trade had been outlawed in Britain in 1807, but slavery itself still continued. William Wilberforce led a campaign to abolish slavery altogether, and in 1823 Thomas Buxton asked Parliament to grant freedom to all children born of slaves. George Canning, the foreign secretary, agreed that ultimately slaves should be freed, and a policy of 'melioration' was begun, starting with a recommendation for the abolition of flogging of women and of the use of the lash in field work in the West Indies. The plantation owners greatly objected to these moves, and argued that they would cause insurrection. A slave rising took place in Demerara in 1823, which was suppressed with great harshness by the planters who argued that English missionaries had incited the slaves to rebellion. This detail suggests that the story is therefore set sometime after 1823 and before emancipation which took place in 1833.

14. *carding-mill*: Mill where wool or cotton was passed through carding machines to comb it ready for spinning or weaving.

15. *ratafias*: Kind of cake or biscuit either flavoured with ratafia, a cordial made from fruits and their kernels (usually almond, peach, apricot or cherry), or designed to be eaten with it. See also *The Mill on the Floss*: 'You are going to change Minny's diet, and give him three ratafias soaked in a dessert-spoonful of cream daily?' (Bk. VI, ch. 1).

16. *peripateia*: More commonly 'peripeteia', a sudden change of fortune or reversal of circumstances; a defining characteristic of tragedy in Aristotle's *Poetics*.

17. *'Lalla Rookh,' the 'Corsair,' and the 'Siege of Corinth'*: Lalla Rookh, subtitled 'An Oriental Romance', was a popular oriental ballad by Thomas Moore (1817); *The Corsair* (1814) and *The Siege of Corinth* (1816) were by Byron. Both poets helped create fashionable interest in the Orient. In Charlotte Brontë's *Jane Eyre* (1847), Blanche Ingram is clearly thinking of *The Corsair* when she claims that the most desirable man is a 'Levantine pirate' (II, ch. 3).

18. *the 'bulbul'*: Kind of thrush greatly admired for its song in the East, and often referred to as the nightingale of the East. It figured in the *Arabian Nights*, and oriental ballads. Thomas Moore, by association, was known as the 'Irish bulbul', see *Lalla Rookh*, 'Twas like the notes, half ecstasy, half pain/ the bulbul utters, ere her soul depart' (ll. 280–81).

19. *spavin*: Form of swelling or tumour in a horse's hock joints.

20. *top-booted*: Top-boots were high boots with a light coloured top (imitating the time when boots were turned over at the top). Although worn by the gentry in the eighteenth century, by the nineteenth century they had lost their

privileged status and were worn by grooms and coachmen as well as upper-class huntsmen.

21. *renegade*: One who deserts one party or principle for another, and in religious terms, particularly a Christian who becomes a Muslim, as suggested here by the turban and crescent.

22. *garbled*: To weed out undesirable items, to make selections from, or mutilate an account with a view to misrepresentation.

23. *division of labour*: The division of social tasks into increasingly specialized roles. The term was popularized by Adam Smith in *An Enquiry into the Nature and Causes of the Wealth of Nations* (1776), and played a central role in nineteenth-century political economy and social theory, particularly in the work of Spencer.

24. *calcareous*: Containing lime (calcium). Lewes, in his articles on 'Food and Drink' in *Blackwood's Edinburgh Magazine*, argued that a certain amount of sugar is good for you: 'The lactic acid formed from sugar dissolves phosphate of lime, and this, as we know, is the principal ingredient of bones and teeth. By its dissolution it becomes accessible to the bones and teeth; and as sugar effects this, its utility is vindicated' (collected in *The Physiology of Common Life*, I, 141).

25. *young lady of the 'Spectator's' acquaintance*: The *Spectator* of 15 July 1712 published a letter purporting to come from one Sabina Rentfree, who had developed a passion for eating old tobacco pipes, stones and coal, before being cured by marriage. She proposes a whole series of names for this malady (including 'Trash-eaters' and 'Pipe-champers') and begs the editor to do his utmost 'to prevent (by exposing) this unaccountable Folly, so prevailing among the young ones of our Sex,' (*The Spectator*, ed. Henry Morley (London: George Routledge and Sons, n.d.), p. 620).

26. *Desdemonas*: In Shakespeare's *Othello*, Desdemona was charmed by Othello's accounts of his adventures (I, iii, 128–70).

27. *Creole heiress*: Creole could denote either a person of mixed race, or simply someone born and naturalized in the West Indies. Thackeray's *Vanity Fair* (1848) briefly features a West Indian heiress, Miss Swartz, who is also described as a 'mulatto' (see chapters 20–21). Bertha Mason, the 'mad wife' in *Jane Eyre*, is also a Creole heiress.

28. *mercer*: Dealer in textiles, particularly silks, velvets and other costly materials.

29. *overseer of the poor*: Until the 1834 Poor Law Amendment, overseers would have been solely responsible for distributing, or denying, parish relief to the poor and for finding the able-bodied employment. Complaints against them were legion. Mr Freely's dedication to doing 'what was good for people in the end' suggests that he subscribed to the doctrines that were to be enshrined in the new law, which sought to make poor relief as difficult and as unpleasant as

possible, under the belief that charity sapped enterprise and initiative.

30. *flat and stale*: Comic linking of this prosaic character with Hamlet:

How weary, stale, flat, and unprofitable
Seem to me all the uses of this world ... (I. ii. 133–4)

31. *Ideal ... Real*: The capital letters were added for the Cabinet edition. Herbert Spencer had written two articles on 'Personal Beauty' in the *Leader* (1854), during the period of his intense involvement with Eliot, where he had defined the Ideal according to Greek sculpture, and picked on some of Eliot's most prominent features to illustrate ugliness (see Gordon Haight, *George Eliot: A Biography* (Oxford: Oxford University Press, 1968), p. 115). Eliot had, understandably, been very hurt by these articles, and became even more preoccupied by her own sense of a lack of ideal beauty.

32. *crop*: For women, shoulder-length curls which were allowed to hang freely.

33. *murrain*: Highly infectious disease of cattle, of which there were repeated outbreaks in the nineteenth century. In *The Mill on the Floss*, Mr Tulliver notes of his unfortunate brother-in-law, Mr Moss, that 'if murrain and blight were abroad [he] was sure to have his share of them' (Bk. I, ch. 8).

34. *gazetteers*: Geographical guides to different regions, which in the nineteenth century would commonly list eminent local figures, as well as the population figures and main employments.

35. *Robinson Crusoe or Captain Cook*: Crusoe is the fictional hero of Daniel Defoe's novel (1719), and hence not a 'public character'. James Cook (1728–79), the first man to circumnavigate and chart New Zealand, also surveyed the east coast of Australia and claimed it for Britain (1768–71). In subsequent voyages he explored the Antarctic, visited Tahiti and the New Hebrides, and discovered New Caledonia. On his last voyage he was murdered in Hawaii.

36. *Mangnall's Questions*: *Mangnall's Questions: Historical and Miscellaneous Questions for the Use of Young People* by Richmal Mangnall (1769–1820), first published anonymously in 1800, soon became a staple of school teaching. See *Middlemarch*, where Mrs Vincy looks down on Mrs Garth for having been a teacher, 'in which case an intimacy with Lindley Murray and Mangnall's Questions was something like a draper's discrimination of calico trade-marks' (Bk. III, ch. 23).

37. *'Without thee ... sweet to die'*: No doubt an adaptation on Mr Freely's part, possibly from a hymn. See, for example, verse 8 from 'Evening II' in John Keble's *The Christian Year* (1827), suggested by Mudford: (Everyman edn) 'Abide with me from morn till eve,/ For without Thee I cannot live:/ Abide with me when night is nigh,/ For without Thee I dare not die.' In her subsequent novels Eliot frequently invented supposed old ballads or poems for the epigraphs to her chapters.

38. *wool-factor*: Wool merchant.
39. *gig*: Light, two-wheeled carriage drawn by a single horse.
40. *liquorice*: The sticks, when steeped in water, were used for medicinal purposes, particularly coughs and sore throats.
41. *K.C.B.*: Knight Commander of the Bath.
42. *Nelson*: Horatio Nelson (1785–1805), commander of the British Fleet which defeated the French at Trafalgar (1805). He was much commemorated in portraits and engravings which, as in this case, faithfully depicted the loss of his right eye and arm.
43. *Titian's colouring*: Tiziano Vecellio (*c.* 1488–1576), the great Venetian painter who used very rich colouring, and revolutionized oil techniques.
44. *the great Leviathan*: Monster of the sea in Hebrew poetry. See Job 41: 1–2: 'Canst thou draw out leviathan with an hook? or his tongue with a cord which thou lettest down? Canst thou put an hook into his nose? or bore his jaw through with a thorn?' The term was also used of a wealthy man, and by Hobbes in *Leviathan* (1651) to define the commonwealth or political state.
45. *head*: *Cornhill* read 'nose'.

CHAPTER 3

1. *sharper*: Swindler, one who takes advantage of the simplicity of others.
2. *Fate's*: Capital added for the Cabinet edition.
3. *cherry . . . lip*: Play upon the saying 'There's many a slip 'twixt cup and lip'.
4. *stale*: Handle.
5. *travelled men*: In *Cornhill*, 'men of extensive knowledge'.
6. *Botany Bay*: Settlement in Australia to which convicts were deported.
7. *peculium*: In Roman law, the property a father allowed his child to hold as his own, by extension private property, and in this case payment for the rights David Faux held in his business.
8. *Nemesis*: In Greek myth the goddess of retribution and vengeance.

APPENDIX

Illustrations for 'Brother Jacob'

'Brother Jacob' was accompanied by two illustrations by Charles Swain on its original publication in the *Cornhill Magazine*. The first, 'Mother's Guineas', which depicts David trying to convince Jacob that buried guineas will turn in to lozenges, was a full-page illustration which acted as a frontispiece to the entire volume. The second illustration, an initial letter drawing, places at the beginning of the tale the scene of David's final nemesis, when Jacob destroys David's marriage plans and carefully-constructed social identity. The illustrations were not reproduced in Blackwood's Cabinet Edition of Eliot's works.